MW00878304

**JOE LEE ROGER**

# THE AGE OF DISCOVERY SERIES

*Volume I*

The Travels and Adventures of Marco Polo
Throughout China and the Mongol Empire

# CONTENTS

# INTRODUCTION

I was switching gears to park the car in front of my place when I saw my daughter's eyes in the rear-view mirror. I gaped when I saw that her face was covered in tears beading down her cheeks. We were coming home after a four-hour drive from a short trip, which, though splendid, was certainly not very eventful. We were coming home to a condo we had on the fourth floor with a fabulous river view facing west, jam-packed with toys and games, state-of-the-art TVs, and a stereo with built-in-the-walls speakers, plus a jacuzzi (a speaker on top of it too). We lived across the street from a wonderful open-air Italian restaurant (red-and-white checkered tablecloths and all), where the owner and staff knew her by name and she could order any pizza, lemonade, or gelato without paying (Daddy's good for it). And we were a five-minute walk from the beautiful town center, which had wonderful gardens and fountains where she would ride her bike, skateboard, roller skates, or simply play with the scores of friends she had living nearby (often until midnight in the summer months). And then a two-minute-walk in the other direction was the River Park (offering similar joys). So, what the hell was wrong with that kid?

1

I guess she must have expected precisely that kind of question from me, perhaps asked in frustration (it happens, I know I'll never qualify for dad-of-the-year). Instead, when our eyes met in the mirror, she had one of those rare moments of immediate understanding, where you feel something that you can't explain with even a thousand words, but the person across knows exactly where you're at and you don't need to say a thing. I knew what she felt because I have felt it myself countless of times: trip's over, back to normal. Though I cannot complain about my upbringing, the environment I grew up in was certainly not better than hers for reasons I don't intend to dwell on here. But ever since I was a kid, I always felt sadness when I would return home from a trip. And I am not talking about a joyful vacation only, for I have had trips that were far from it. I have hitchhiked, jumped cargo trains, slept rough, walked miles on end in torrential rain, suffered dehydration, starvation, nasty insect bites, injuries, food poisonings, and moonshine hangovers. I have lived and worked in primitive conditions with even more primitive people in prison-like environments. On different occasions I have been mugged, shown closely the inside of the barrel of a gun, beaten up, and left for dead; I have survived weather, fights, and crashes. Yet, I have always felt an overwhelming joy and excitement when I would go on a trip, especially to somewhere I had never been to; and I would always feel that little sadness when the trip is over and I return home (full disclosure here: I can barely fit into that jacuzzi, but my daughter and her sleep-over friends tend to have lots of fun in it).

Well, it's the 21st century and we have four-wheel drives, paved roads, petrol stations, hospitals, helicopters, mountain rescue, police stations, GPS and internet coverage, vast amounts of free knowledge at the tip of our fingers, insect and animal repellents, modern anti-allergic, antiseptic, anti-fever and anti-what-not medicines; we've mapped every corner of the planet and we can practically google-translate a conversation into a language we have just learned exists. We travel at speeds and costs that were not considered possible less than a century ago (and we can have a whisky on the rocks on the way or a mahi mahi). Still, if you were to try and cross Eurasia, following in the footsteps of Marco Polo, you will find it more challenging than you ever thought (and please don't go through Afghanistan). In truth, he must have had that same travel bug my family seems to be suffering from. Surely the freedom of travel, the sense of adventure, the thirst for knowledge and the joy of seeing or first-hand experiencing new things all far outweigh the inconveniences and dangers of traveling. But was that the case nearly eight centuries ago?

Nowadays, if we were to undertake such a trip, we would conduct thorough research using the internet and the comforts of our own home, we would purchase all sorts of medicines in advance, know what climate we'll experience and prepare the right clothing for it, know what places to avoid, and we will most likely have an itinerary with tickets purchased in advance. In the 13th century, they did not even have maps (and the ones I've seen were pretty useless); they did not know where they were going and what they were getting themselves into; they did not have credit cards that could be hidden under your shoe sole,

3

and they treated all illnesses with leeches. Yet, undisputedly, there were men (mostly it was men) brave enough to make the first step, men that were attracted by the risks of jumping into the unknown, and men who, one by one, brought about invaluable knowledge of routes and places previously unknown, unimaginable opportunities for trade and expansion, and above all, made the world more aware of itself.

Most of the great explorers associated with the Age of Discovery were Europeans and there were objective historical, technological and geopolitical reasons for this; most of them were seafarers. It is widely accepted that the Age of Discovery began in the 15th century, when the Portuguese set out to explore the Atlantic (outside of the Mediterranean Sea) under the sponsorship of Prince Henry, known as Henry the Navigator. But I will start 150 years before that. Because when one talks about travel, adventures, and explorers, one name immediately comes to mind almost by default:

## Marco Polo

Everyone has heard of Marco Polo. He was that amazing traveler from all of those centuries ago, and he had adventures and battles and love affairs, and he was handsome. All you have to do is watch the series on Netflix or perhaps some of them oldies if that's your thing. Unfortunately, most of the dramatizations about Marco Polo are far from reality. His depiction in modern times is at total odds with the man himself. History can be gray, if it isn't lit up by a rainbow of drama and artistic license. That doesn't mean it cannot still be interesting and entertaining.

While he may not be the dashing Gary Cooper portrayal of an earlier cinema version, he was still a man rich in stories and conquests that hardly seem possible in the 21st century. This was a man who lived a life beyond anything that even closely resembled mediocrity.

Born in Venice in 1254 – a Republic of Venice that is unrecognizable today – he was raised in what was one of the largest financial centers of the world, with one of the highest per capita GDP and arguably the strongest naval force, if not globally, then certainly in the Western world. The access to the sea, its huge port and the number of traders that arrived on a daily basis, made Venice an easy place for a young man to learn languages, become cosmopolitan, and master the mercantile trade.

His father and uncle, Niccolo and Maffeo, were absent for the first fifteen years of his life as they were both traveling through Asia to increase their family wealth through trading. When they returned – and actually got to see young Marco for the first time – they all three soon embarked on the journey that ultimately defined Marco Polo's life. They traveled the Silk Road – as important as a trade route then as it is a desirable tourist route today – as they made their way to Cathay (a previous name for what we now regard as northern China) and returned by sea. They were received by the Royal Court of Kublai Khan, and it was Marco who impressed the Khan and became his special envoy.

Marco stayed in the kingdom for over seventeen years, traveling far and wide, as well as exploring the inner country of what today we call China. It was these incredible journeys that made up the manuscripts that followed, now regularly referred to in modern times (in English) as 'Marco Polo's Travels.' By this time, Marco in particular had become important to the Royal Court, and the Khan had initially refused to allow him and his relatives to leave. Eventually though, permission was granted. After nearly two decades of travel, which at times seemed almost unbelievable, the Polos accompanied the Mongol princess, Kokochin, to Persia, where she was to marry the Ilkhan[1]. It took them around two years to arrive and most of their travel companions did not make it, so that in itself was a remarkable journey.

After leaving her there (mission accomplished), they eventually returned to Venice after a 24-year absence, at a time when the city was at war with the Republic of Genoa. It's worth reflecting at this moment, they had traveled in the region of 15,000 miles (or 24,000 kilometers) and had returned with a fortune in gemstones. Marco immediately joined the conflict, and financed the arming of a galleon with a slingshot device called a trebuchet: it's an incredibly deadly and highly successful weapon that the Polos introduced into China and Kublai Khan used to conquer the last remaining stronghold of the Song dynasty. Polo was captured in 1298 off the Anatolia coast and spent approximately three years in prison. It was here that he narrated his adventures to a fellow inmate, who went by the name of Rustichello da Pisa. He was a romance writer who liked to add his own interpretations and

---

[1] That is how the ruler of Persia, which was called the Ilkhanate in those days, was referred to.

personal experiences to the manuscripts. This, although the original is now long lost and forgotten, became the base for the book previously mentioned, which has of course been the inspiration for so many portrayals of Polo in modern culture. Christopher Columbus himself carried a copy of it on his historic voyage to America two centuries later.

Once released from prison, Marco married Donata Badoer, the daughter of a well-known merchant, and fathered three daughters. He died at the age of 70 in 1324 as an extremely wealthy man who bequeathed a lot of it to his family, but also gave some to convents and religious institutions. The exact time of death – or indeed date – can never be determined, as Venetian law stated that the day always ended at sunset, no matter when that came. It is believed it was on either the 8th or 9th of January 1324.

One more interesting story attached to Marco Polo, in a life that defined the word, was that he told an astrologer that he had seen a star 'shaped like a sack' in the sky one night when he was returning from the Sea of China. This was almost certainly a comet, something which at the time was regarded as a far more spiritual event than today, but there were no comets recorded at the time he said he saw it. Researchers, much later, have established that there was one in 1294, but interestingly this event – which even today would be a moment worth noting – was never included in his manuscripts.

Marco Polo was not a womanizer, who taught Chinese women how to kiss; they certainly knew a lot more about intimacy than any European, who was supposed to be ashamed and confess to a priest after just thinking about it. Nor was he a battle expert, who taught the Chinese army how to use gunpowder as it is shown in films; they invented it and had been in possession of it for 250 years before he showed up. He was, however, one of the world's greatest travelers, one who opened up Asia to the European mind. He was also one of the greatest merchant traders of all time. Adding to that, an emissary, a writer and a prisoner ... and there is so much more to learn about a man whose image is now being molded into a completely different visage.

The book that brought fame and notoriety to Marco Polo was originally called Livres des Merveilles du Monde, meaning 'Description of the World,' although it wasn't a book at all. It was originally a set of translated manuscripts, which with everything that concerns historical documents, has been changed and misinterpreted ever since.

The original manuscripts have disappeared from existence, and scholars now rely on numerous versions in numerous languages, the most accurate appearing to be the version in Franco/Venetian. Franco is a very old French which bears hardly any resemblance to the language spoken today, and the Venetian was the version of the Italian language of the day. There are also versions in Latin and Tuscan, and each different translation appears to be a different version of events. Some copies were also heavily censored by Catholic priests who clearly did not want certain wonders of the East to reach the good (or not so good) Catholic public.

The book – as we can now call it, even though it is divided into four parts – was dictated by Marco Polo to his prison cellmate, the romance writer Rustichello da Pisa, whilst they were held prisoner in Genoa. While Marco Polo attempted to provide an elaborate and factual account of his travels, Rustichello was a romantic writer, and the early versions clearly mirror his previous writings, so that the events described appear to have an extravagant and imagined viewpoint. This has caused scholars, historians and experts down the centuries to question how much of the book is true and accurate.

In fact, some doubt that Polo even actually visited China. For example, there is no mention of the Great Wall of China, which in the 13th century was still highly visible, even if the various walls (there are actually more than one) were in a state of serious disrepair. Critics have suggested that he took the version of Cathay (China) from his father, who had visited years earlier. As someone who has traveled to China myself, it seems inconceivable that this mighty structure was not mentioned anywhere, as it is visible in many parts of the country. Then again, it is plausible that the wall at the time was more of a series of fortifications, mostly in a bad state of disrepair, as they were no longer needed; and the contiguous great wall we most visit today was yet to be built by the Ming Dynasty after expelling the Mongols. Besides, Polo does state that he did not share many things he saw because people would not believe them. Whatever the controversies surrounding the book, which become more and more numerous as the years passed, it has given an incredible insight to the Far East in the 13th century.

The first attempt to serialize the manuscripts into a volume of works took place in Venice in 1559 by Giovani Battista Ramusio, who collated the works from the 14th century. He described them as being "perfectly correct." A later version called Marco Polo Il Milione (the nickname Milione was given to him after he returned to Venice and constantly repeated that Kublai Khan's wealth could be counted in millions...) added another 140 manuscripts found in the archives for a printing in 1871. The first English version was printed by John Frampton 1579, whilst an extended book, which also included a 700th anniversary celebration, was released in 1960.

The book has, of course, changed throughout the years. Its current word count of around 110,000 is manageable and can either be engaging or amusing, depending on your point of view, but it is incredibly important as a history tool. It has also managed to create the image of the man that we now see as Marco Polo, although it's debatable whether that image has remained accurate to his real-life portrayal or not.

Despite this, Marco Polo's book provided just about the most comprehensive contemporary description of China and the Mongol Empire. At the time, this spanned almost the entire Asian promontory, except for the sparsely inhabited Russian north, the Levantine coast, and the southern peninsulas (admittedly large in landmass and people). The Mongol Empire controlled the important land routes that facilitated trade between East and West, colloquially known as 'The Silk Road.' At this point, trade over The Silk Road had been going on for centuries, but there were essentially no written accounts about it and few people would've traveled through its entirety; merchants would rather sell their (uninsured) wares to trade posts closer to home rather than risk them being stolen in foreign lands. Back then, it wasn't even known as 'The Silk Road,' but enterprising people and striving empires were very aware of its existence. To understand the importance of Marco Polo's life work, we need to first understand the importance of the phenomena known as The Silk Road.

# CHAPTER I

# THE SILK ROAD

Ah, the Silk Road! Such an exotic destination for those who want to go slightly further afield. It's the 'bucket list' addition that many people want to tick off, yet few rarely do. For those that pay the large fees, you can travel along part of the original route (or routes) that had merchants and traders deal in fabrics, jewels, and of course, silk, all of those centuries ago, except it isn't quite like that. Like the Great Wall of China, there is more than one road, and the original has almost been lost in time, replaced by sea routes and other easier options. In fact, many scholars now prefer to call it 'Silk Routes,' which appears to be far more accurate, if not all that practical. There's a hitch though.

The name of 'The Silk Road' only existed from 1877, when it was coined by German explorer Ferdinand Von Richthofen, who made seven expeditions to China between 1868 and 1872. This is despite the fact that the original road was effectively abandoned and unused for around 400 years. At no stage during its 1,500 years existence was it referred to as 'The Silk Road,' and certainly not by Marco Polo, who made it far more famous in the 13th century than ever before. Still, it is now the accepted name for a trade route that has developed over time into the main highway for trade between East and West.

The history of the original route, which spanned over 4,000 miles (6,400 kilometers) is as fascinating as it is lengthy, so where to start but at the beginning.

In 138 BC, the second Chinese imperial dynasty – the Hans – was looking for allies against the "barbaric" but powerful northern tribes, which they referred to as the Xiongnu (a Turkic tribal confederation, part of which migrated west later on and became known as "the Huns" in Europe). Emperor Wu sent an envoy named Zhang Qian to look for potential allies in the west, and Zhang became the first person to describe the vast expanses of Central Asia for the Chinese. Over the course of 20 years, trade was firmly established between the Han dynasty and the Greco-Bactrian Kingdom, which spanned Central Asia. Having begun the warfare against the Xiongnu in 133 BC, the Chinese needed stronger horses for their armies as their horses were brought up in inferior land and terrain, so their bones and legs were weak. This meant they weren't able to carry soldiers and their arms for long periods or distances while the horses from the Steppe, used by the Xiongnu, were of superior quality. So much so that Chinese soldiers would exchange silk or jade from the mines of Yarkand and Khotan (in northern China) for the stronger horses they needed from the Xiongnu at the foot of the Great Wall of China; this was a 'black market' exchange, something that the Han dynasty wanted to end for obvious reasons.

Emperor Wu was particularly impressed by the Dayuan horses of the Fergana Valley (dubbed the 'heavenly horses' by Qian)

13

and wanted to use them against the Xiongnu. Trade was initially refused by the Dayuan because they had good relations with the Xiongnu whose lands were near their border; they also figured that the Han were far away across deserts that were difficult for an army to traverse. Hence, they represented no threat. Except Emperor Wu begged to differ! In 104 BC, he sent general Li Guangli to subjugate the Dayuan in what became known as the War of Heavenly Horses. He was unsuccessful at first, but a second expedition was organized in 102 BC, which resulted in the Han successfully conquering the Dayuan and securing the supply of heavenly horses for their army. This opened the door for Chinese expansion into Central Asia and placed a nascent Silk Road under the Han dynasty. The road crossed over from the Eighteen Provinces of Inner China through the Hexi Corridor and the Tarim Basin, then onward to the Fergana Valley, in the easternmost part of what we now call Uzbekistan. It also helped them win the war against the Xiongnu, though it did continue for over a decade after that.

It was at this time that the road linked up to a road network in Persia that had existed for roughly the previous three centuries. It was started under Darius I of the Achaemenid Empire four centuries prior and initially linked Susa (in modern-day western Iran) to Sardis (in modern-day western Turkey). It was a massive undertaking for its time and Herodotus wrote that nothing traveled faster than the Persian couriers; his praise for the messengers "neither snow, nor rain, nor heat, nor gloom of night stays these couriers from the swift completion of their appointed rounds" has become the credo of the modern US Postal Service. The Royal Road was later extended into a network of additional (if smaller) roads, which helped trade, communication, policing, and tax collection in the Achaemenid Empire. They reached Alexandria in Northern Africa, Persian ports on the Arabian Sea, and the Ganges River in the Indian Subcontinent; more importantly for the Silk Road, they reached Samarkand and Bukhara in Central Asia, which found themselves in the Greco-Bactrian Kingdom three centuries later and so connected with the Chinese trade routes.

That is how the Silk Road was born, although it wouldn't be known as the 'Silk Road' for another 20 centuries. The Silk Road was not just a route that gave people the chance to trade and barter with merchants. As we will see, cultures were defined by the routes, with heritages and beliefs being transported along the road, to be landed in a foreign land that would embrace a new and different way of living. But it wasn't all positive, as the Road also carried armies and diseases like the Black Plague.

By 30 BC, the Roman Empire had extended to such a level, that they had taken control of the western parts of the Silk Road. In fact, Roman soldiers, acting as mercenaries, had fought alongside the Iranian forces in the battle of Sogdiana in 36 BC. Some historians suggest that the crossbow, used in a spectacular way by the Roman Empire, was actually the result of trade between China's Han dynasty and these very same soldiers, as the weapon had long been used by the Chinese Army.

All told, Roman citizens obtained access to the enormous wealth and jewels that came about from trading with the Chinese. By selling their own glassware, foodstuffs, and artifacts, then bargaining for the heavily desired Chinese silk, they could enjoy

15

a luxury that had not previously been seen by any Empire up until that point. It's quite an interesting and rather amusing fact, that the Romans thought that the Chinese silk came from trees and believed that the reason for its superiority was that silk trees only existed in China! And the Chinese didn't bother them with production details, for fear of losing such a lucrative trade. Chinese silk was just about the most important currency available, alongside gold and jade. At one point, it was almost banned in the Roman Empire. The official reason for this was decency, as it enabled women to dress very provocatively; however, the reality was that it had begun to cause a deficit in gold within the empire.

The Chinese kept the making of silk a hard secret, and even in the 6th century, there was still that belief that it grew on special trees that could only be found in that area. It wasn't until the Byzantine Empire grew, as a continuation of the Roman Empire and made its base in Constantinople, that the truth was finally revealed. Emperor Justinian the Great had been told that two monks had discovered the secret of silk production, and so he ordered the same two Nestorian Christian monks to travel the route and steal the silkworm eggs that produced the fine silk. This they managed to do, and so the silk production was no longer entirely the preserve of the Chinese, but now was made in northern Greece for the Byzantine Empire.

But silk was not the only commodity traded from East to West. Two of the most important commodities that had a profound effect on western civilisation and history were gunpowder and paper; the West was also hungry for spices, dies, porcelain, teas, medicines, and other goods. At the same time, the Chinese hungered for armor, horse wares, glassware, furs, honey, certain animals and foods, textiles, rugs, and others.

The Silk Road was often closed due to conflicts, mostly involving the Chinese Dynasties. There is a temptation here to look upon such events with a 21st century point of view. Surely, it was so vast and long that it wouldn't be possible to close the whole route. Surely travelers could still use it, and traders could still trade? They could, but at their own peril. The road traversed vast barren lands where human occupation was barely seen. For a caravan of travellers to attempt to travel along it would be risky at best and suicidal at worst. And it is easy to see that it is one thing to take your valuable and uninsured merchandise to an established and secure trading post via a policed road; it is quite another to take it unlawfully hoping you may find somebody to purchase it before it gets seized by law enforcers or bandits. When the road was closed, it was patrolled by armies, with barely a soul allowed to pass. Trading stopped, and so the comparative wealth of the West and the East was affected. When it was open, communities grew and 'watering holes' and trading posts existed, so trade was easy to conduct and profit from.

The Silk Road also brought together cultures, isolated tribes, and various faiths, all attracted by the prosperity offered by trading, and the benefits of an integrated society. Religions spread, beliefs were questioned, communities reached out to each other, and life became more prosperous than before. Both Buddhism and Islam were directed towards China through traveling along the route. There were also downsides, such as diseases, which had previously never been seen in a certain community and would tear it apart since no immune system had built up yet. Conflicts were rare though. The Silk Road was at its peak, and like dominant Empires, there never seemed to be a time in the future when it wouldn't be so.

By the 8th century, the route was becoming dominated by Islam as a faith. Islamic rule expanded rapidly at first by conquest in Arabia, North Africa, and the Middle East, where the Umayyad Caliphate was established in 661 CE. And the Silk Road was the main conduit for establishing it throughout Persia and Central Asia by trade, missionaries and cultural exchange[2]. Islam, as a set of cultural norms and religious beliefs, thrives in all those regions to date. There was a dark side to this exchange too; in the 9th century, it brought Turkic mercenaries from within Central Asia into Persia and the Middle East. These lands were already part of the Abbasid Caliphate, which succeeded the Umayyad Caliphate in 750 CE. This proved to be fundamental for the history of the entire Middle East and Europe, which sparked a chain of events that had important consequences for our book so I'll briefly describe them.

The mercenaries in question were known as Mamluks, which is the Arab word for slaves, as the bulk of this army constituted men either captured in war or purchased as slaves. They were brought in as a private army by al-Ma'mun, the seventh Abbasid caliph, brought under the command of al-Ma'mun's half-brother al-Mu'tasim bi Ilah, and used successfully in various military

---

[2] Contrary to popular belief, the Islamic religion was not forced on the locals; the ruling elite were Muslims but the locals were only gradually converted to Islam.

18

campaigns. Unfortunately for the Caliphate, it turned out that these mercenaries were only loyal to gold; and even more unfortunately, they were a force to be reckoned with. Long story short, their presence eventually destabilized the Abbasid Caliphate and brought about its fragmentation and internal strife over the course of a mere 50 years. This weakening of the Caliphate opened the door to the Buyids, former vassals, who conquered west Persia and in 945 took over Baghdad, subjugated the Caliph, and made him their vassal. Then came the Fatimids, who by 970 had conquered Egypt, Syria, and both shores of the Red Sea (Mecca and Medina included), and had started vying for influence in Baghdad, promoting their own caliph. Then came the Seljuk Turks, who ran over Persia from within Central Asia (again) and captured Baghdad in 1055. The Seljuks thus became de facto rulers of the Caliphate and after a period of relative calm, started a conquest of Anatolia that spelled doom for the Byzantine empire, who proved unable to put up a fight. Most of the peninsula fell into Seljuk hands within a decade or so. So desperate was the situation that the Byzantine emperor Alexios I Komnenos cried for help from the Pope in Rome, despite the Great Schism between the Orthodox and the Roman-Catholic churches.

The menace to Christianity in the Straits invoked the Pope to act and this started the Crusades in 1095 CE. The crusaders inflicted a massive disruption upon the newly forming Seljuk empire, which at the time controlled much of the Middle East, Persia, and Anatolia. The Crusades were successful at first and took over the Levantine coast, to protect the Holy Lands, but they also proved to be quite expensive and difficult to support, once established, so their presence proved precarious and gradually declined. Still, a century later, at the turn of the 1200s (or in the times of the Polos), there was firm Christian presence in the Levant, the Seljuk empire was stifled and fractured, and the Abbasid Caliphate had regained control of a small piece of land (but was a shadow of its former self).

Then, something else came from the East.

# CHAPTER II
# THE RISE OF
# THE MONGOL EMPIRE

## Genghis Khan

If you were to take a straw poll on any street in any city, and ask if they could name three great Empires in history, then it's pretty guaranteed that the Roman Empire would be the first. That's mainly because the two words go together, even if many people have only a cursory knowledge of the history and rely on modern-day media retelling of the story. The British Empire would almost certainly be mentioned, especially in the English-speaking realm, and then it would be a little more difficult. The war in Ukraine may invoke some to remember the Russian Empire, some may mention Spain, others Holland (or The Netherlands), and maybe some would veer towards China, but very, very few would mention the Mongol Empire. This is quite extraordinary, given that between the 13th and 14th centuries, this was the largest empire in the history of the world.

If you think of the Mongol Empire, then you have to think of Genghis Khan. A figure in history that has probably been dramatized far more than most, who has been portrayed by numerous actors in movies in modern times, meaning that the true character of the man has gradually been lost in time. Most people associate Genghis Khan and the Mongols with brutal conquest, savagery, and oppression, and are then surprised to hear from historians that the Mongol Empire was, for its time, quite a tolerant undertaking, where other religions and cultures were treated with respect and which was administratively run largely by foreigners; mind you, that was happening a century and a half before the Spanish Tribunal of the Holy Office of the Inquisition was established and seven centuries before the "master race" concept.

Genghis Khan was born into the Borjigin clan to Yesugei, a chieftain descended from warlord Bodonchar Mungkak, perhaps in 1162[3]. He was given the name of Temujin by his father, who used the name of the Tatar chief Temujin-uge, a general he had recently captured. Yesugei had betrothed his son to a girl from the prestigious Ongirrat tribe and had traveled with him to meet his future bride, Borte, before leaving him there to work off the large dowry. It was when he returned home alone that he took advantage of a band of Tatars hospitality – something which was expected, as well as accepted – but they recognised him and slipped poison into his food. His father died shortly afterwards.

The details of Genghis's life that followed are sketchy to say the least. After his father was killed, his clan followers scattered, and it was the mother, Hoelun, who took on the duty of protecting

---

[3] It's almost impossible to gain an accurate description of his early years. Even his birth date is a matter of conjecture, with a date of 1162 widely acknowledged; but even that is disputed, as some historians give dates as far apart as 1155 and 1167!

her family and children. This involved taking them to the Khentii Mountains, where they apparently lived off the land. There are three events that define his early childhood, though. The first is that Temujin killed his half-brother Begter for stealing a fish, the second is that he was captured by the Taychiud tribe and lived in a cage before managing to escape, and the last was that he became the blood brother of the Mongol military and political leader, Jamukha. That effectively paved the pathway for his future.

In 1177, his bride, now wife, was captured and held captive by the Merkit clan, presumably for ransom. In what became a feature of his life, Temujin attained the help of 20,000 men to recapture and release her. This was done with minimal violence, but showed that at an early age, he had already managed to attract the following of many supporters. There were numerous skirmishes between the Merkits and his clan down the years, but as historians have struggled to isolate individual battles, it's difficult to establish where and when.

It's the year 1206 that really brought about his rise to power, as it was in that year that he became Genghis Khan, and officially proclaimed the existence of the Mongol Empire. This came about by the subjugating and uniting the clans of the Merkits, Naimans, Mongols, Keraites, Tatars, and Uyghurs (and by wiping out the ones that didn't join). They were brought together as one political and warring faction, overseen by Genghis, who was now the most powerful leader in the world. The pledge to him as a leader was written by the chieftains of the various disparate tribes, and reads as such:

23

*"We will make you Khan. You shall ride at our head, against our foes. We will throw ourselves like lightning against our enemies. We will bring you their finest women and girls, their rich tents like palaces."*

At the same time, the Chinese state of Xia, which was situated just south of the Mongol lands and was the domain of the Tangut dynasty, had become significantly weakened following the disposing of Emperor Xuanzong. The Khan led a raid into Western Xia, where he sacked Wuhai, the main garrison along the Yellow River, and invaded the Ordos region. This gave him and the Mongol Empire direct access to the northern reaches of the 'Silk Road,' especially with the caravan routes that had become extremely lucrative. A year later, he launched another campaign against Western Xia, capturing several more cities along the Yellow River, but then came his first serious setback. The fortress Kiemen held the only passable access through the Helan Mountains to the capital Yinchuan. This was guarded by approximately 150,000 soldiers, and the Mongol army was nowhere near large enough or equipped well enough to take the battle, so he retreated briefly.

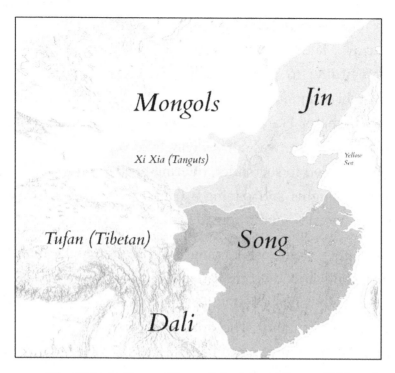

*The Chinese Dynasties and the Mongols – c. 1206*

It's worth noting here that the Mongols lacked expertise in siege battles. They didn't have the ability to take the walls of the Tangut dynasty since they couldn't build siege weapons. Their strength had always been their ability to fire arrows at long distances with exactitude, even more remarkable as they were able to do this on charging horses that they controlled only by their legs. Their only tactic in a siege was to set their camp outside the walls and effectively surround a city, then hope to starve it into submission. Peasants could not go out to gather the crops and soldiers could not go out to fight the superior Mongol cavalry. But the Mongols could not breach the walls, so if the city was well stocked, it was an impasse.

For six months, between May and November, Genghis Khan and his army laid siege, even at one stage attempting (unsuccessfully) to divert the Yellow River to flood the city. Emperor Li Anquan sent envoys asking for help from the Jin dynasty Emperor Wanyan Yongji, but was flatly refused because the Mongol menace was not yet widely recognised. In the end, Li Anquan decided to surrender, offering his daughter, Chaka, as a token for Genghis and paying a tribute of textiles and camels. After that, word began to spread.

The Mongols were fast gaining a reputation with both their fighting skills and the brutal treatment of those who opposed them; but in cities that did surrender, life continued in comparative normality. The option to surrender was far more desirable than attempting to beat the most powerful and battle-hardened cavalry in the land. When capturing a city, the Mongols took special care and made much use of local leaders, scholars, medics, and craftsmen; those included Chinese engineers who helped them finally build siege weapons. The combination of Mongol warriors with Chinese weaponry and technology created a force that swept through the lands of the Tangut dynasty like a juggernaut. And in March 1211 CE, they came knocking on the door of the Jin dynasty.

The Jin was a much larger state that was situated in North-East China. It included Manchuria and the northern basin of the Yellow River. The Mongols invaded with a cavalry force of 90,000 against the Jin's elite cavalry of 150,000. And their infantry of 800,000! The attack came from the west-northwest against the Jin Dynasty's Great Wall, which was built to repel Mongol attacks[4]. The wall had battlements and castles dotted along its entire route, but it was more a system of separate fortifications rather than a continuous wall as we tend to imagine. And Jin General Wanyan Chenyu, who was charged with its defense, ordered his troops to spread out along its entire length and as they spread thin, their numerical advantage vanished. Genghis Khan, well informed by the scores of scouts he sent, attacked at the least defended spot at the fortress of Wusha. This fortress led to a desert ridge, inhabited by wild foxes and duly named Yehuling, or "Wild Fox Ridge". The advantage of taking that ridge was the fact that it led straight to Juyong pass, which was the gateway to Jin's capital, Zhongdu, which today we call Beijing. Genghis took the Wusha fortress with relative ease, but the Jin army scrambled quickly to defend the Wild Fox Ridge while the Mongols were recuperating. The mountainous terrain made it hard for the Mongols as they had to fight on foot, but the Jin forces were spread thin along the ridge's length and had poor communication between them. Genghis was also helped by the defection of a Jin emissary Shimo Ming'an, who, realizing that he was clearly now on the wrong side of the battle, immediately provided him with important military intelligence. So, the Mongols eventually prevailed in what became known as the battle of Wild Fox Ridge, which opened the way to Zhongdu (Beijing). The city fell after a four-year long siege, during which the capital's residents had to resort to firing silver and gold with their cannons (after metal reserves were exhausted), and to

---

[4] What we refer to as the Great Wall of China was not yet fully built at the time. The place where the Mongols attacked is referred to by historians as the Jin Dynasty's Great Wall. The bulk of the Great Wall of China that tourists see today was built by the Ming dynasty in the 13th century, more than 150 years after these events.

cannibalism to survive (after food reserves were exhausted). Zhongdu was captured and sacked, forcing Emperor Xuanzong, who had retreated with his courtiers to the southern city of Kaifeng, to become Genghis's vassal. The Jin dynasty couldn't possibly survive such a humiliation, and over the course of the next twenty years, the empire completely collapsed.

## Expanding West

The Mongol Empire was now extending its power beyond anything seen before. To the west, a small force of 20,000 soldiers managed to pursue, capture, and execute the former Khan of the Naimans, Kuchlug, who had previously fought without success against Genghis Khan. The Naimans were subjugated in 1204, but Kuchlug was still considered a threat. He fought again with Genghis in 1208, leading remnants of the Naiman tribe, but was pushed further to the west. He then fled to the emperor Yelu Zhilugu of the Western Liao dynasty, who ruled what was then known as Qara Khitai (modern-day Xinyang, northeast Uzbekistan, and southern Kazakhstan). By 1211, Kuchlug had married the emperor's daughter Princes Hunhu and had deposed her father off the throne with the help of Muhammad II, ruler of the nearby Khwarezmian Empire (more of which in a moment). In 1216, after the successful Jin campaign, Genghis Khan sent his general Jebe to subdue Kuchlug since he had gotten too much power for his liking. Jebe's victory against a 30,000 Qara Khitai force meant that the Mongol Empire now had control as far west as Lake Balkhash in southern Kazakhstan.

What followed then was an extraordinary event in the rise of Genghis Khan and the Mongol Empire.

In the 13th century, the area that we now know commonly as Uzbekistan, Turkmenistan, Western Afghanistan, and Iran, was ruled by the Khwarazmian dynasty, and had been since 1077. It was one of the largest dynasties in the area, and of course Genghis Khan eyed it with desire. He didn't immediately go to battle, though, as he initially preferred a trading alliance along the Silk Road, so he sent a 500-man caravan to establish ties with the then Emperor Ala-ad Din Mohammad II. This was loaded with gold and silver, plus textiles and fabrics for trade. Unfortunately for him and the dynasty, the governor of the city of Otrar ordered the caravan to be attacked as he thought there were spies as part of the group. If ever someone made a wrong choice, then it was probably the governor Inalchuq, who history has now blamed for the catastrophically bad decision. What followed was inevitable, especially as three ambassadors, who had been sent to complain about the attack to the Shah (two were Mongols and one was a Muslim), were shaved and beheaded. Hell has no fury, and so Genghis's hordes went on a rampage.

Firstly, Genghis Khan deployed around 100,000 of his best soldiers and had them cross the treacherous Altai Mountains in winter. This has been compared to the infamous Hannibal crossing of the Alps, especially since it was winter and there was heavy snow on the route. It was equally as devastating in terms of casualties, but enough of the fighting army survived to conduct a surprise attack with around 20,000 men. This confused the Shah, showing how much of a military tactician Genghis was, despite his infamy now being almost exclusively because of his brutality in battle.

The Shah, unsure if this was the main Mongol force, sent his army to meet the Mongols, but Genghis had sent a secondary force to besiege the city of Otrar. The battle actually carried on for over five months, but only when a citizen, clearly in fear of his life, opened the gates to the walled city and the Mongols stormed in, did it finally end. The Mongols laid ruin to the buildings and executed many of the citizens and inhabitants, torturing and pillaging along the way. The governor was executed too, and the city very quickly became part of the Mongol Empire. Next was the city of Bukhara. This wasn't heavily fortified, so the conquest was reasonably easy, but the 'justice' handed out to the citizens was as brutal as could be imagined. Many were tortured and executed. Others were forced to join the Mongol army, whilst a large proportion were employed as slaves. This was the Genghis Khan that we now know.

He had actually entered the city himself, something which was unusual for an Emperor, and he brought all the city's aristocrats and elite to a mosque, then lectured them. He told them that if they hadn't sinned, then God would not have sent a punishment like him to them. He then had them publicly executed.

Samarkand in Central Asia was next. The Khan's new military tactic, which he used to great effect, was to hold prisoners as body shields. Once the battle was won, in reasonably quick time, he executed every remaining soldier who had fought against him, displaying their severed heads at the gates of the city. The men and women were taken out of the city, divided into groups of gender, and then were slaughtered too. That is the common understanding of what happened, but scholars have disputed this now with a lack of archaeological evidence. There is now a suggestion that it didn't happen in Samarkand, but rather in Nishapur, and came about when the Khan's son-in-law was killed by an arrow. His bereaved wife and Genghis's widowed daughter, who was also pregnant at the time, was given the duty of announcing the punishment for such an act. She decided that as well as killing all of the city's people, every dog, cat and any kind of animal should be slaughtered too, so there would be no living thing left in the city (though I very much doubt they accomplished the task as far as rats and roaches were concerned).

The Shah fled and only the city of Urgench remained in the hands of the Khwarazmians. This inescapably fell too, but the resistance was far greater than before. Inevitably, victory came and the usual executing of the population followed, with those who remained being forced into slavery. Again, historical sources diverge here. It was said that each Mongol soldier, of the 50,000 that had fought, were told to kill 24 citizens each. That would have resulted in around 1.2 million executions, but these numbers don't really stand strong as facts. Even so, it was another brutal butchery of a city that had been taken by Genghis Khan's Mongol Empire. All told, Khwarazm, an empire that ruled Persia and most of Central Asia, and stood strong for 150 years, ceased to exist in less than three[5].

---

[5] Technically, there was a small territory remaining in western Persia and there were attempts to re-establish the Khwarazmian Empire by Muhammad II's son, Jalal al-Din Mangburni, but this was a shaky affair with constant infighting, which ended in 1231.

By capturing Northern China, Central Asia, and Persia, Genghis and the Mongol Empire now controlled the 'Silk Road.' Political centers were strewn along the route, such as Zhongdu in China (which the Mongols called Khanbaliq, or the Khan's city), Karakorum in Central Mongolia, Samarkand in Transoxiana, and Tabriz in Northern Iran. From what was a loosely connected and fractured area, it created a political unity and unification like never before. Surprisingly, the control of the route was done in a benign way, as other cultures and beliefs were accepted, and goods, technology, and trade were free-flowing, completely at odds with the image we have of the unforgiving Genghis and his Empire. It united Chinese, Persians, Mongols, and Arabs, as well as the faiths of Tengrists, Buddhists, and Muslims. It also made the Mongol Empire the richest in the world, and despite their traditional nomadic lifestyle, they would take advantage of the labor and the talent they found each time in the conquered lands, using that labor and talent for the furtherment of their cause; they essentially embraced the people they had subjugated. For one and a half centuries, the roads and the routes were run by the Mongols, creating what historians refer to as Pax Mongolica.

After the very quick fall of Khwarazm, the conquests continued. In what was an enormously savage period, Genghis raided Afghanistan with around 20,000 of his soldiers, whilst a second army – now under the control of the Khan's main generals Subutai and Jebe – raided both Armenia and Azerbaijan. The Mongols then overran Georgia, sacked and destroyed the important trading port of Caffa (now known as Theodosia), and crossed the Caucasus mountains to the north. Exhausted from the crossing, which happened during the winter, Subutai's army was met by a 50,000 strong allied force of Alans, Cumans[6], Lezgins, and Volga Bulgarians. The Mongol army was at first repelled and the allies stood their ground, reasoning that the Mongols, pressed against the mountains and low on supplies, would simply die of starvation or leave. Subutai, however, managed to bribe the leaders of the largest force against him, the Cumans, and they left the alliance. Having defeated the remaining force against them, Subutai and Jebe then chased the traitor Cumans across all of the northern Caucasus until they reached them near the Don River and (no surprise here) slaughtered them.

The plains they were riding across felt like home, only warmer and richer. The Mongol army sacked the city of Astrakhan, at the mouth of the River Volga on the Caspian Sea, with relative ease and then proceeded west across the Don River. Subutai and Jebe split their forces, with Jebe riding further west to the Dnieper River, while Subutai took a turn south to the Crimea. It was about this time that a link between the Mongols and the Venetians was first established. The details are murky, but when general Subutai reached Soldaia, the Venetian trading post in Crimea, he decided to enter an alliance, promising to destroy any non-Venetian trading posts in Crimea. Knowledge was an invaluable commodity in those days and the Venetians, these vulnerable merchants, gave Subutai a chance to learn a lot about Europe; knowledge, including military intelligence, that his Khan would greatly appreciate. Besides, the Mongols had learned from the Chinese that the best way to amass wealth is not by raiding, but

---

[6] The proper term should be Cuman-Kipchaks, since they represented both tribes in a Cuman-Kipchak confederation, which had existed since the 10th century, but I will deface them and use Cumans for short throughout the book.

33

by trading, and I guess they saw that despite their small numbers and the vast distance from their home, the Venetians were extremely good at it.

The Venetians seem to be the only people Subutai treated favorably. Otherwise, he enforced the harshest possible punishment on enemies that opposed him. And he got ever more creative at that. Having taken a beating, the Cumans went to the princes of the Rus principalities to the north – Smolensk, Kiev, Chernigov, Galicia – and formed a union against the Mongols that mustered a 60,000 strong cavalry force to expel them from their lands. After sending emissaries to the Slavic princes for a state of peace, Subutai was incensed when they were executed and peace was rejected. The Russians felt superior and chased the smaller Mongol force (at the insistence of the Cumans) east across the Dnieper River. The Mongols gave the appearance that they were running, but it was a tactical retreat. During this nine-day chase, they were constantly harassing the Russian-Cuman force with hit-and-run tactics, so the forces were spread thin, with the Cumans riding a day ahead and the Russian princes riding detached from each other as separate battle groups with Mstislav III of Kiev, who advised caution, coming in last. The Mongols, Cumans, and some of the Russian vanguards crossed the Kalka River (which terminates at Mariupol in modern-day Ukraine), at which point the Mongols turned and slaughtered everything in their path. They then crossed back and started picking off the Russian princes one by one, giving them little to no chance of fighting. Mstislav III was the only one who could manage some semblance of defense by arranging food wagons in a circle; it held for three days until they ran out of water. After the Battle of the Kalka

River, 90% of the combined Cuman-Russian forces survived. Mstislav III and the rest of the Russian nobles were placed under a wooden platform, upon which the Mongol generals had themselves a soiree while the Russians were slowly crushed to death underneath. To this day, I still wonder if it was a good thing that they didn't have DJs back then, as it would have made their death more painful, but quicker.

There were no lands conquered during this two-year raid in the Rus even though Subutai managed to defeat every horse-tribe, army, or capital standing in his way, pillaging Georgia, Astrakhan, Crimea, and destroying the armies of the Rus nobles. The Mongols just passed through. There was some profit and treasure to be gained, but Genghis Khan was more interested in knowledge of the lands and peoples that inhabited the area, so this became, in effect, the goriest research field trip the world has ever seen.

In 1226, Genghis attacked the combined remnants of the dynasties of the Tanguts in Western Xia and the now demoralized Jin dynasty, which were becoming restless and refused to contribute to the Mongol campaigns. Genghis Khan first focused on the Tanguts, easily taking the cities of Heisui and Ganzhou. That was followed by the Western Liang, one of the sixteen states of China. Despite strong and brave resistance from the Tanguts, the Khan and his forces overwhelmed any army that faced them. They took the important industrial city of Lingzhou before crossing the Yellow River once more, and it was here that legend says Genghis Khan saw five stars aligned in the sky, believing it to be an omen for his future success. It seemed to be correct, as in the following spring, his army then continued to advance forwards, taking the Xining and Deshum provinces, followed by the Qingshui and Gansu provinces. The Tangut generals actually surrendered to him after the latest humiliating defeat, but in time-honored fashion, Genghis just put them and the princes to death for resisting in battle.

On the 25th of August 1227, the most brutal and successful of warriors died. The Mongol Empire had attracted attention throughout the world now, most notably in Europe, where their advances were of great concern, but the Khan's death came as a shock. There are so many different versions and explanations of his death that the truth is now almost impossible to establish. Some had him being shot and killed by an arrow in another battle with the Western Xia, others have him falling from his horse and eventually dying from his injuries, Marco Polo suggested that Genghis Khan died from the infection from a wound, but a recent study – as recent as 2012 – makes the strong claim that he died from the bubonic plague, which was affecting the Mongol army at that time. Whatever the cause, the great Khan was dead.

As was the custom of the time, he was buried in an unmarked grave, which is now almost impossible to establish. He was returned to his ancestral home of Khantil Armag in Mongolia, and to hide the fact that he had died, his army slaughtered anyone who was in the path of the procession, so as to keep it a secret. Brutality to the end.

# CHAPTER III
# SUCCESSES AND SUCCESSIONS

## The Succession of Ögedei

Genghis Khan's third son, Ögedei, was nominated by his father as his successor, which happened before the siege of Otrar in 1219 as Empress Yesui[7] insisted that a successor be picked before the war with Khwarazm. There was a furious fight between Genghis's first son Jochi and his second son Chagatai, and seeing that choosing either of them would cause an irreversible rift in the Empire, Genghis named Ögedei as successor. He had fought alongside his father in many battles and was decreed as the obvious person to continue the expansion that the Mongols had started a decade ago. But as Ögedei and Chagatai were closer to each other than Jochi (they led the siege of Otrar together), this replacement caused a rift between Jochi and the rest of the family that would later prove detrimental for the Empire.

---

[7] She was his third wife and a sister of his second wife; Genghis married the third at the insistence of the second. Some people …

While Ögedei was named the Great Khan, the other three sons of Genghis were promised their own khanates, provided that they remain loyal to the Great Khan and keep the Empire united. Jochi had died six months before Genghis, and so his sons, Orda and Batu, received the western steppes, which at the time reached the Ural Mountains; they split the land with Orda, heading what became known as the White Horde in the east, and Batu heading what became known as the Blue Horde in the west[8]. The second son, Chagatai, received the territories where most of today's Central Asian countries lie. The fourth son, Tolui, was given the old Mongolian homelands. Ögedei's own khanate spanned China and Eastern Mongolia. And he had every intention of expanding it.

One of the most important battles that Ögedei started was the total invasion of Korea, or as it was known then – Goryeo. There had been many skirmishes between the Mongols and the Goryeo dynasty through the years, but the peninsular state still stood strong.

Between August 1231 and January 1232, the Mongols set about to completely overwhelm the Korean forces. The army was placed under the leadership of General Saritai, and they immediately crossed the Yalu River, taking the strategic North Korean town of Uiju. There then followed an unusual and frustrating defeat for the Mongol army, as the Siege of Kuju against the Goryeo was lost. In a tactical masterclass, though, Saritai bypassed the remaining Goryeon soldiers and then took

---

[8] Those names were supposedly derived from the color of their yurts, which during wartime were changed to golden color.

the capital city of Kaesong, which even today is a major industrial hub of North Korea.

The Goryeon generals, acutely aware of the importance of the city, called for peace, but as ever with the Mongols, peace came at a price. They demanded 10,000 otter skins, 20,000 horses, 10,000 bolts of silk, clothing for one million soldiers, and the delivery of women and children, who would subsequently become slaves in the Mongol Empire. The Koreans, still not totally under the control of the Mongols, made plans for the evacuation of their citizens as a way of ensuring their safety. Most of the population, and the Royal Court, was moved to an island in the southern area of Korea, called Ganghwa. Here they felt relatively safe, as the one part of attack that the Mongols were weak at was attacking by sea. They hadn't mastered seafaring ways, and so an island in the middle of the Han River offered peace. This, of course, brought about a second invasion by the Mongols, but it was a total failure (or Charlie Foxtrot in the parlance of the US military). They couldn't reach the island, and the general who had had so much success, Saritai, was killed by a monk during the battle. A third invasion was now planned.

One cannot accuse the Mongols of not being persistent. There wasn't just a third invasion, or a fourth or a fifth; there were seven further invasions over the next two decades, showing how difficult it was for the Mongols to break down the defenses of Korea and explaining why it remained independent of the vast Chinese Empire to date. It wasn't until around 1270, long after Ögedei's death, that the battles were effectively over, with the Goryeons devastated by the continual bombardments.

Apparently there wasn't a single wooden structure left standing as the result of the regular incursions into their territory. Once the battle had been won, Kublai Khan (who became the Great Khan in 1260) made the announcement that Goryeon was *"a country that long ago even Tang Taizong personally campaigned against but was unable to defeat, but now the crown prince comes to me. It is the will of heaven."*

During Ögedei's rule, the invasion of Russia, by an army of around 40,000 soldiers, became another remarkable account of the sheer willpower and stamina of the Mongol Empire. The campaign was led by Batu (Jochi's second son), the forces were commanded by Mongol general Subutai (who had seen these lands as we know), and Ögedei's sons, Guyuk and Kadan, also took part (although the former appeared to be regarded as a weak leader who constantly criticized his own men). It took place in the winter of 1240, and it actually took place at that time deliberately! The Mongols decided it would be far easier to advance when the lakes and the rivers were frozen over; and besides, few would expect soldiers to march in areas where the temperatures were below freezing and the snow was feet thick. For some idea of how remarkable this was, recall the Napoleon campaign, six centuries of military science and technological development later, when his soldiers attempted to capture Moscow, but the freezing temperatures defeated them. They came from the west where the winter is far less harsh and food supply is a lot easier than in the east (a.k.a. Siberia). This was the scale of the victory over Russia! Kiev and Chernigov were captured, and many smaller towns and cities were invaded, and became part of Mongol rule. Russia's Kievan Rus was breaking up, and stayed under Mongol rule for at least two centuries until Moscow (or as it was known, the Grand Duchy of Muscovy) began its independence struggle.

After capturing all of the Russo-Ukrainian steppe, Batu and Subutai advanced further west. Parts of Europe that were invaded and subjugated were Poland, Hungary, Croatia, Bulgaria, and the Latin Empire in Constantinople, but by 1242, the advances came to an end with Ögedei Khan's death. The Mongols retreated east of the Carpathians with most of them heading towards Mongolia to take part in the kurultai, the ceremony where the next great khan was to be elected. Batu Khan, however, unlike his brother Orda, chose not to return to Mongolia. Instead, he established his headquarters in Sarai (formerly the Khazar capital Atil), on the Volga River just northwest of the Caspian Sea. He subsequently became known as the ruler of the Golden Horde, named due to the fact that in wartime, the yurts that he used were a golden (and not blue) color. His domain stretched from the Chu River in modern-day northern Kyrgyzstan in the east to the Carpathian Mountains in the west; and the Second Bulgarian Empire, which spanned most of the Balkans, had become his vassal state during the Mongol retreat from Europe. The Golden Horde was supposedly a joint khanate between the Blue Horde in the west and the White Horde in the east, but the western part quickly took prominence and Orda Khan in the east did not seem to mind.

The Mongol retreat from Europe was put down to, in later years especially, Ögedei's alcoholism. He had always appeared to be a humble man who declined any suggestions that he had greatness about him. To a father's son, who constantly attempted to live up to the ideals and successes of his father, drinking became a comfort. It had been noted by his courtiers and generals that in accord with their wishes, he agreed to cut down the number of cups of alcohol he would drink in one day. Unknown to them, though, he doubled the size of the cups. He died at dawn on 11th December 1241, and even that was not without its different explanations. Some say that he had been so affected by the death of his brother Tolui that he became morose and uncommunicative, but as that had taken place nine years previously, it seems unlikely. Others say that he attempted to make a pact with God, promising to release a captive animal if God would cleanse his bowels from the alcohol. It obviously didn't work. He died after an all-night drinking session with one of his generals. If you were ever hungover from kumis (traditional Mongolian fermented mare's milk[9]), you would know he was spared one hell of a hangover.

By the time of his death in 1241, Ögedei had made extraordinary administrative reforms throughout the empire, including the introduction of civil service, paper currency, postal service, and taxation. This was no doubt helped by the bright, educated minds from conquered lands that were now voluntarily working for the Empire, their culture and religion tolerated and respected by law. He had conquered much of Korea and penetrated deep into Song territory, while the Mongol armies had taken over Russia, Georgia, and Ukraine, and had reached all the way to Poland, Hungary, and Bulgaria, ravaging all three kingdoms in 1241 (and making Bulgaria a vassal state). In fact, it is argued

---

[9] It is lighter than some beers actually, but although the taste is weird, once you start, it is hard to stop. As with beer though, the hangover is nasty.

that it was Ögedei's death that stopped the Mongolian war machine from reaching all the way to the Atlantic even as Pope Gregory IX was calling for a crusade against the Mongols.

## The Toluid Wars

The Empire's ultimate fracturing, however, was already in sight. The years after Ögedei's death were marked by instability and succession struggles until Möngke Khan (a son of Tolui, the fourth son of Genghis Khan) rose to power ten years later. He managed to overthrow the House of Ögedei with the help of Batu Khan of the Golden Horde. Möngke Khan oversaw another great administrative reform, one part of which was giving his two brothers, Kublai and Hulagu, powers as local heads in China and Persia, respectively. This no doubt improved the efficiency of management but was yet another step towards the ultimate and fatal divisions in the empire.

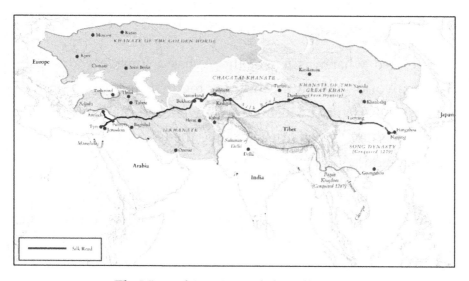

*The Mongol Empire and the Silk Road*

43

In 1256, two years after Marco Polo was born, Hulagu began campaigns in the Middle East, which effectively began the end of the Caliphate and, historians argue, the Golden Age of Islam. He eventually conquered the biggest and most prosperous city of Baghdad, after a mere ten-day siege (followed by a seven-day sacking, where only the Christian population was spared). Marco Polo describes Baghdad as the city where the caliph of all Saracens sits, just like the head of all Christians sits in Rome. The city was blessed with a great river that linked it directly to the Indian Ocean and was accordingly one of the most prosperous and largest markets. So rich was the caliph that he had a great tower filled to the brim with gems, gold, and silver. Upon discovering the tower, Hulagu, who had never before seen such wealth amassed in one place, asked why didn't the caliph use at least some of it to gather knights and mercenaries to defend the city from him? As the caliph had no good explanation, Hulagu locked him in the tower and ordered his guards that the caliph was only allowed to eat or drink his treasure; he died four days later.

This ended what was left of the Abbasid Empire and left the Islamic world without a caliph for the first time. As he turned against the Ayyubid Muslims, who were the rulers of Syria, he was helped by Christian parties like the Georgians, Armenians, and Crusaders.

In 1259, though, Möngke Khan died of sickness during a campaign against the Song dynasty in China. It happened around the same time that his brother Hulagu had just taken over all of Syria. Realizing that his brothers Kublai and Ariq would attempt

44

to take advantage, Hulagu hurried back, taking most of his army with him. The Mamluk sultan Qutuz, who resided in Cairo, exploited this and moved on Palestine against the Christians and what was left of the Mongols. Outnumbering them two-to-one, Qutuz managed to crush the Mongol-Christian force at the battle of Ain Jalut and killed around a third of them before the rest fled. The Mamluks, now the largest Muslim power, would capture Damascus within a week. Sultan Qutuz, however, did not live too long to enjoy it, as under two months later, he was murdered by Baibars, who proclaimed himself the sultan. Baibars remains known to history as the sultan that started the era of Mamluk dominance in the Levant, drove out the crusaders of King Louis IX of France (the Seventh Crusade), and led the armies that inflicted the first material defeat of the Mongols. This was a turning point in Mongol history as it coincided with the strife and division already taking place in the Far East.

The youngest brother of Möngke Khan, Ariq, proclaimed himself Great Khan in the capital, Karakoram, and received the support of the nobles. His elder brothers were far away, Hulagu fighting in the Middle East, and Kublai in southern China. In addition, Kublai was a Buddhist and as such considered too weak at times and too close to the Chinese for the liking of Mongol traditionalists. According to some historians, Kublai was not in Möngke's favor as he often demanded greater autonomy for the Chinese realm and Ariq was Möngke's successor of choice. Kublai, however, declared himself Khan, marched north to Karakoram, and started a civil war; at the same time, Hulagu went on his way to Mongolia with the intent to support his older brother. Simultaneously, Berke Khan, their cousin who became the leader of the Golden Horde after his brother Batu's death, decided to support Ariq. He attacked to the south and began raiding Persia (or the Ilkhanate as it was called by the Mongols). Berke was a converted Muslim, who was outraged by the news of the sacking of Baghdad, and he also had old grievances to settle with Hulagu. Berke considered the lands of the Ilkhanate to be within the realm of Jochi's succession and saw Hulagu as a usurper of power within these lands.

In 1260, Hulagu joined forces with Kublai in what became known as the 'Toluid Civil War,' which lasted for four years. Kublai captured Karakorum, while Ariq's forces were absent, and razed it to the ground. At the same time, his march to the north allowed the Song dynasty to claim back territories it had previously lost, while northern China, part of the Mongolian Empire for decades, became restive with parts of it in open rebellion. Kublai, dependent on supplies from China, was forced to turn back south, while at the same time Hulagu was forced to return west to the Ilkhanate and face Berke and the Golden Horde. He successfully pushed them out of the Ilkhanate but subsequent campaigns in the lands of the Horde, led by Hulagu and his son, Abaqa, ended in defeat. In the end, the borders remained where they were.

Kublai managed to pacify China, not by suppression but by negotiation, tax reduction, and also by portraying traditionalist Ariq as an enemy to the Chinese and a usurper of power. He began encroaching on Ariq, who had taken back Karakoram, by cutting off the supply lines to the capital in an encirclement that spanned almost the entirety of China. Ariq, meanwhile, succeeded in placing Alghu, Chagatai's grandson and a protégé of his, as khan of the Chagatai Khanate in Central Asia, thus gaining a powerful potential ally. Kublai did not engage Ariq directly, preferring instead to surround his realm and cut supplies off. In the occasional times when Kublai's and Ariq's forces actually engaged in battle, Kublai's generals inevitably proved superior, and soon some of Ariq's allies began turning against him. When the situation became untenable, Ariq appealed to the Chagatai Khanate to help him militarily, but Alghu refused. Ariq reasoned that while his brother was still engaged in China, he could march on Alghu, but that gamble proved fatal as Alghu defeated Ariq's army and he lost the last few remaining allies he had. Ariq then traveled alone to Xanadu, Kublai's newly established capital, just north of present-day Beijing, where he surrendered himself in 1264, was imprisoned, and died mysteriously a few years later (some say by poisoning).

With Ariq now gone, Berke recognized Kublai as Great Khan, but that recognition was mostly formal. The following year saw the deaths of Hulagu of the Ilkhanate (after several days of banqueting), Berke of the Golden Horde (while raiding the Ilkhanate after Hulagu's death) and Alghu of the Chagatai Khanate (while warring with Kaidu of the house of Ögedei on behalf of Kublai Khan). Kublai named the new Ilkhan to be Abaqa, Hulagu's son, and Möngke Temur, grandson of Batu Khan, as leader of the Golden Horde. Kublai remained a Great Khan only in name, but continued the Mongol expansion, ruled over China, and founded the Yuan dynasty in 1271, which was certainly a testament to his increasingly strengthening affiliation to the Chinese; over the course of his rule, he established a system of public schools, introduced paper money backed by silver, turned previously established post stations into trading posts, and vastly increased the exchange of goods and ideas borne by the Silk Road. The Chagatai Khanate in Central Asia and Afghanistan remained independent of Kublai and ruled by Chagatai's line. The Golden Horde in the lands of the Rus was ruled by the line of Jochi and adopted Islam as its religion under Berke's ancestors' leadership; it was never truly beholden to the Great Khan. The Ilkhanate in the Middle East, Persia, and western Afghanistan (like the Yuan dynasty in China) was ruled by the blood line of Tolui, but was marked by constant infighting and instability and, following a few unsuccessful attempts at a Franco-Mongol alliance to rout the Mamluks, it eventually also succumbed to Islam.

It was in these tumultuous times when Marco Polo's father and uncle, Niccolo and Maffeo, traveled into the Mongolian empire and met with Kublai Khan. And their journey started in a place where the Orient and the Occident have always met.

# CHAPTER IV
# CONSTANTINOPLE

## The Fourth Crusade

The story of Marco Polo begins with his father Niccolo and his uncle Maffeo Polo, as it was their exploits that eventually put him on this historical epic journey of discovery. They were born around 1230 and became quite successful Venetian merchants at a time when Venice's power was greatly expanding and its per capita wealth was perhaps the greatest in Europe. They had both become involved in business well before Marco was born, and indeed it is entirely possible that neither brother was aware of Marco's existence at the time of their first major journey. This cannot be confirmed, but it is known that they missed the first fifteen years of his life, and he did not see his father or uncle during that time. His mother died when he was five and so Marco was brought up by an aunt.

The two brothers left their home in Venice in 1253, a year before Marco's birth, for the huge city of Constantinople, the largest trading center in Europe at the time. As Venetians, they enjoyed diplomatic immunity, plus tax relief in Constantinople, due to their country's role in establishing the Latin Empire during the Fourth Crusade in 1204. How this came to be bears importance to the story of the Polo brothers, so I will try to briefly narrate an otherwise extremely complicated affair.

The fact was that the Venetians had a special relationship with Constantinople all the way back to 1082 when Alexios I Komnenos issued a golden bull (a special imperial decree) that granted the Venetian merchants rights to free trading, tax exemptions, and control of the main harbor in Constantinople. The Byzantine Empire's finances and navy at the time were exhausted by wars with the Normans (Vikings) that controlled southern Italy. It was vulnerable in the Adriatic Sea and needed Venice's powerful navy to help protect its western coasts. This is how the Venetian quarter in Constantinople came to be, but this also started growing resentment between Orthodox Christian denizens of Constantinople and the 'Latins' (a few decades later treaties with similar effects were granted by Manuel I Komnenos to the merchant republics of Pisa and Genoa). The locals watched for the good part of a century as the Latin merchants were given more and more rights and privileges, getting rich, and bribing officials to bend the rules in their favor, building expensive estates and treating the locals with undisguised disdain, as second-hand subjects.

Things came to a head in 1182 when in an attempt to seize power from the queen regent Maria of Antioch, Andronikos I Komnenos stirred local anti-Latin sentiment into a bloody riot; he used the fact that she was of French origin and has recently further expanded privileges to the Latin merchants. It was one of the city's bloodiest moments as the crowd slaughtered

50

thousands of Latin merchants and sold off the survivors to the Seljuk Turks as slaves. There was subsequently a gradual restoration of relations with Venice, as the Byzantines needed their ships, but things remained tense.

Then, in 1204, the Venetians came back with a vengeance.

In 1198, newly elected Pope Innocent III, began calling for a fourth crusade to free Jerusalem from Muslim hands (as the third one failed). Despite succession strife in the Holy Roman Empire and a war between England and France, an army of volunteers was gathered under the leadership of Theobald III of Champagne. In 1200, Theobald went to Venice to arrange the building of a fleet to ferry what was expected to be an army of 4,500 mounted knights, 9,000 squires and 20,000 lightweight soldiers (including archers). For Venice, apart from the hefty payment for building the fleet and transporting the army, that also meant prestige, new allies, and access to new ports (where the Genoese were prevalent); it also negotiated to get half of the plunder. So Venice agreed to hold off all its commercial enterprises for a year and prioritize the building of the fleet as well as to supply the army with food for nine months.

While the fleet was being built, however, Theobald died and with all the conflicts in Europe, it proved hard for the crusaders to find a replacement. Finally, Boniface of Montferrat, an Italian, agreed to it, but gathering the French knights under his banner proved problematic. Many of them left for the Holy Lands by their own means and from different ports, such as Calais and Apulia, and as a result, only about 12,000 people showed up in Venice. As they could not cover payment by a wide margin, the

Venetians offered them to sack the Dalmatian port of Zara, which used to be part of Venice but had been taken by Hungary 20 years prior. This was a Catholic port, so many of the crusaders angrily refused and left. The majority agreed to the plan, though, and were joined by a 20,000 strong Venetian force, so Zara fell in short order, creating an unheard-of precedent of a crusading army sacking a Catholic city.

As the Pope excommunicated the crusaders for this, the army continued breaking apart and there were even armed clashes between the crusaders and the Venetians. Boniface, in search of new recruits, went to his cousin Philip of Swabia. At the time, Philip was harboring his brother-in-law, Alexios IV Angelos, who was an heir to the throne of Byzantium. His uncle Alexios III had usurped the throne, while his father Isaac II was out campaigning (unsuccessfully) against Bulgaria. Isaac II himself came to power by usurping the throne from Andronikos I Komnenos while the latter was away campaigning (unsuccessfully) against the Kingdom of Sicily. That was the same Andronikos who had sparked the anti-Latin riot in 1182 and usurped the throne from Maria of Antioch while she was campaigning (unsuccessfully) for the support of the Greek population against her stepdaughter, who also vied for the throne. If you notice a pattern in Byzantine succession traditions, it's because there is one. Unlike Andronikos who suffered a horrible three days of public ordeal before he finally perished, Isaac II was alive, though blinded and in prison[10]. Alexios IV wanted justice and promised the crusaders

---

[10] Blinding was considered a merciful sentence in those days. It was done because blind people could not hold administrative positions of power. So if one was afraid of a potential rival to the throne but did not want to execute their rival, they would blind them (and I guess feel slightly incensed if the blinded person did not thank them).

200,000 golden marks (more than double what they owed the Venetians), 10,000 men to help them take Jerusalem, and, above all, to place the Eastern Orthodox Church under the primacy of the Pope. This last promise secured Pope Innocent III's blessing and the withdrawal of his excommunication.

The battle for Constantinople was epic and it was in fact the Venetians who first succeeded in breaching the lightly fortified sea wall. This was the largest amphibious assault in medieval history. The ships were specially designed by the Venetians to quickly land the mounted heavily armed crusaders, and they disembarked north of Galata. The crusaders breached the Galata fortress and removed the chain that was guarding the Golden Horn harbor situated between Galata to its north and Constantinople to its south. They then proceeded inland, around the Golden Horn, and attacked the heavily fortified northwestern wall of Constantinople.

The broken chain allowed the Venetians to enter the harbor, destroy Constantinople's defending ships, and attack its (north-northeast facing) sea wall that was lightly fortified by design as there was presumed to be no danger of land forces attacking it; it faced the Golden Horn harbor to its north, and the harbor was secured by the chain crossing from Constantinople to Galata. The bulk of Constantinople's defending force (15,000 strong, of which a third were Varangian guard) was concentrated against the crusaders at the opposite northwestern wall of the city. Having realized that the wall was breached and the city was falling, Alexios III managed to sack the entire treasury of the city and escape with it.

Isaac II was restored as an emperor and confirmed his son's promises would be kept but he needed the crusaders' help in restoring the treasure back from Alexios III. Part of the crusaders left towards Adrianople, where it was presumed Alexios III had taken refuge. The remaining (Latin) knights stayed in Galata, separated from Constantinople by the harbor. The treasury was empty and precious church artifacts were melted by Isaac in order to make some payments to the crusaders and demonstrate good will. Anti-Latin riots broke out because of this. Then as Byzantine tradition heralds, the emperor (and his son) were killed by a cousin named Alexios V Doucas[11], who bribed the Varangian guard to do this (unlike the Crusaders they hadn't been paid anything yet).

It was obvious that Alexios V had no intention (or ability) to honor his predecessors' promises and the crusaders decided that they would take over Constantinople, impose their own emperor and divide the Byzantine lands among themselves. Stationed as they were in Galata, they drew up a contract about Byzantium's partitioning and attacked. The city fell again, not least because the still-unpaid Varangian guards decided to leave; Alexios V fled and that is how the Latin empire was born.

The destruction inflicted on Constantinople was colossal. Half the city's wooden houses were already burned mostly for tactical reasons but that made no difference for the population that was now homeless. The crusaders however had decided to take the city, so they could get what was promised to them in the first

---

[11] There are doubts if Alexios V was in fact a relative to Alexios IV or a descendant of the Komnenos dynasty but this is hardly relevant to the events.

place. Now that the treasury was empty and the leadership and the guards had fled, they began robbing everything that was of any value. Churches were stripped of valuable artifacts, buildings were stripped of metal ornaments, gems, pearls, and ivory items were looted, statues were dismounted and destroyed, palaces and stone households were robbed of everything from marble statues and handcraft furniture to chalices and icons[12]. Emperors' tombs were opened and robbed of anything precious (jewelry, clothing, weapons). But the greatest barbarism was the smelting of countless of giant bronze statues that could be found throughout the city: monuments of Greek and Roman mythology figures and creatures, heroic historical figures, pyramids, weather vanes, animals, humans, sphynxes, colonnades, chariots … all smelted into cheap copper coins.

The only ones who seemed to care about preserving artifacts and works of art were the Venetians. This was not for humanity's sake though; as a nation of merchants, they could easily recognise value and so preferred to keep things that were worth more when not smelted. A bright example in that regard is the world famous quadriga, which can now be found atop St. Mark's Basilica in Venice.

The Venetians became an integral part of the Latin Empire and, in fact, the first emperor, Baldwin of Flanders, was elected with their support. Boniface of Montferrat was the runner-up, supported by the crusaders, but the Venetians had secured a dominant vote in the Council. Boniface was granted lordship over the Kingdom of

---

[12] To their credit, violence over the population was limited (though still occurring). There are accounts of a standing order to execute anybody caught raping for example.

Thessalonica (lands in northern Greece around the lucrative port of present-day Thessaloniki). Venice also received plenty of land: three eights of the empire according to the Partitio terrarum imperii Romaniae as the contract for the partitioning of the Byzantine Empire drawn by the crusaders was called. The doge of Venice, Enrico Dandolo, was the only one who did not have to swear allegiance to the emperor; all other crusaders that received lands were named vassals to the Latin Empire. The contract however entitled rights to lands that the Latin Empire could not practically control (apart from a piece of land in Eastern Thrace).

## The Latin Empire

The Latin Empire all but destroyed the Byzantine economy. Despite the internal instability and customary usurpations, executions and blindings for which Constantinople was infamous, it was the largest trading hub in the world and was renowned for its luxurious image and lifestyle of the nobility. To this day it is known as the crossroads between Europe and Asia. The importance of Constantinople comes from the fact that it sits astride the Bosporus, which is the gateway between the Mediterranean and the Black seas. It was a safe harbor and an excellent port for those that are welcome to sell their merchandise and pay their tax. Commerce over land was not as lucrative because the cost of carrying cargo over land would jump to about one hundred-to-one and the merchant selling it often needed to go through territories that were not always friendly. However, the lands surrounding Constantinople were rich and fertile, which meant that the city could draw upon a large agricultural base (cereal crops, vines, olives around the coastal areas as well as livestock in the mountainous interior). Grain was an important export commodity, but so was silk, for the Byzantine Empire was the only European state that knew how to produce it (thanks to those two Nestorian monks). In the markets of Constantinople one could trade other luxury goods like perfumes, spices and gems but also honey, wax, wine, oil, meat, fish, grains, furs, and salt as well as craftworks like ceramics, glassware, linen, textiles, rugs, jewelry, etc. Sadly, slaves were also on the menu.

As a thriving international market, Constantinople had developed a sophisticated, if corrupt, bureaucracy, but the Latins did not trust the Greeks and decided to replace it with their own. It was a total disaster, which caused a collapse in production and trade. Such was the damage caused that despite the halving of the population (as the homeless fled), the city experienced serious food shortages and arguably the main goods exported from Constantinople became relics that the crusaders had looted (e.g. the Crown of Thorns).

With the partition, it was understood that one quarter of the lands, along with Constantinople, would be directly controlled by the Latin Emperor, one quarter and a half would be controlled by the Doge of Venice and the remainder would be distributed amongst the crusaders, who would remain vassals to the empire. That was on paper but the Byzantine nobles that fled Constantinople had other plans, better knowledge of the land, and were better accepted amongst the locals. Boniface of Monferat was a notable exception as the populace in his realm welcomed his marriage to the widow of Isaac II, Margaret of

Hungary. People actually liked him but Dandolo was against him becoming the Latin Emperor as his lands and relations were too close to Genoa and so he doubted him.

Baldwin I set out to solidify the claims of the empire in Thrace and was at first met with resistance. He also successfully captured Alexios V, the last Greek to make the claim to the Byzantine throne and executed him publicly in Constantinople (by throwing him off the 40-meter-tall Column of Theodosius on the Theodosius Square, which was considered novel and imaginative by the contemporaries).

In the meantime Baldwin's brother Henry went to claim his lands in northwest Anatolia, where he successfully defeated Theodore I Lascaris (son in law of Alexios III Angelos) who had fled Constantinople to the city of Nicaea. Theodore did not engage with the heavily armed crusaders but managed to expand his authority into what became known as the Empire of Nicaea. That very same year he ran into skirmishes with David Komnenos who had established another successor state – the Empire of Trebizond, which mostly expanded along the southern shore of the Black Sea with the help of Georgia. Though few in numbers, the crusaders managed to keep both Anatolian empires at bay but on the Balkans, the situation was different.

In 1205, Bulgaria stirred Greek riots that ended up in the slaughter of the Latin garrisons, left by Baldwin at Adrianople and Didymoteicho. This forced the rapid relocation of crusaders to deal with the threat. The Bulgarian army defeated them outside of Adrianople and captured the emperor Baldwin I; his fate was unclear but he was never seen again. His brother Henry could not reach Thrace on time to help him and was met by the fleeing remnants of the crusaders at Constantinople. He tried to retake the lost fortresses of Adrianople and Didymoteicho, but did not succeed. Boniface would not help him as he was busy campaigning to the south into Thessaly. And then the Bulgarians came back and ravaged all of eastern Thrace, defeating the combined defending forces of crusaders and Venetians and dangerously approaching Constantinople itself.

This created a window of opportunity for Theodore I Lascaris in Anatolia, where he expanded the newly fledged Nicaean Empire to become the dominant force and successor kingdom first at the expense of Trebizond and later the Seljuk Sultanate of Rum. He reached the Bulgarian tsar Kaloyan in 1207 and suggested a joint siege of Constantinople, which was gladly accepted. The joint attack was unsuccessful but the idea was not entirely scrapped.

In the meantime, Boniface had a son, Demetrius, with Margaret of Hungary and his legitimacy among the Greeks was solidifying. He expanded his domain into Thessaly, where people mostly bent the knee without fighting, but it was recognised that he lacked hard military power. Meanwhile to the west, Michael I Komnenos Doukas had solidified authority over the Despotate of Epirus, which quickly became a threat to the Latins. By 1223, Michael's successor and half-brother, the ambitious Theodore Komnenos Doukas, would succeed to expand the Despotate into the lands of Thessaly and take over the Kingdom of Thessalonica with designs to restore the Eastern Roman Empire. He also managed to poison Latin emperor Peter of Courtenay, who succeeded Henry, and to crush a crusading army sent by the Pope Honorius III to stop

Epirus's expansion. In 1229, he allied with Bulgaria with a plan to jointly take over Constantinople from the Latins. However, Theodore also procured the support of Holy Roman Emperor Frederick II (a nemesis of the Pope and by extension of the Latin emperor) and received a massive army of 9,000 German knights to help him against Constantinople. He decided that he could use this force to first dispense with his Bulgarian allies that could later prove a threat to him. Leading this force, he felt so invincible that he actually brought his family to the battlefield. At the battle of Klokotnitsa in 1230, the army of Epirus was crushed along with the German knights, and Theodore Doukas was captured; only Manuel Doukas, his brother, managed to escape with a small contingent.

The new Bulgarian tsar Ivan Assen II commanded respect and was popular amongst other peoples, so Bulgaria annexed all of Epirus lands with little resistance and Ivan Assen II became ruler of almost the entire Balkan Peninsula. Bulgaria helped depose the Serbian king Stefan Radoslav, who supported Theodore Doukas, and replace him with his brother Stefan Vladislav, who supported Ivan Assen II and married his daughter, Beloslava. At this point, correspondence with Nicaea began anew. The only remaining ally of the Latin Empire in the region was the Duchy of Morea, situated on the Peloponnese Peninsula. The Bulgaro-Nicaean alliance laid siege of Constantinople in 1235, but that proved unsuccessful thanks in large part to the Venetian fleet that came on time to protect the Golden Horn from the Nicaean naval forces. John of Brienne, regent to Baldwin II (the juvenile Latin emperor at the time), managed to repulse the Bulgarians despite being heavily outnumbered and there are chroniclers that compare John's valor to the likes of Hector of Troy and Ogier the Dane.

The following few years were marked by an uneasy truce between the Latin Empire and Bulgaria until the Mongols came. As already mentioned, the Mongols, led by Batu Khan, ravaged Poland and Hungary before coming to the Balkans through Croatia and Serbia (who were minor kingdoms at the time). They swept through Bulgaria and reached Constantinople. Baldwin II was the Latin emperor after John of Brienne died in 1237 and he commanded an army he himself raised in France against Nicaea. While it was a considerable force, the Mongols completely annihilated it in Thrace, and Constantinople became a Mongol tributary. But following the death of Ögedei, the Mongols left the realm and Batu Khan founded the Golden Horde with a capital at Sarai on the Volga River (at the time known as Sarai Batu).

In the meantime, a different Mongol force under general Baiju was approaching Anatolia from the Ilkhanate. The Seljuk sultan of Rum, Keyhusrev II, failed to pay homage to Karakoram and Baiju had the task to subjugate the Sultanate. Keyhusrev II gathered a large force comprising men from all the Anatolian kingdoms, including Nicaea and Trebizond, as well as Armenia, Georgia, Latin mercenaries and The Ayyubid kingdom of Aleppo. The Mongol army crushed this force at the battle of Kose Dag and the Sultanate of Rum, along with Trebizond, became tributaries to Karakoram in 1243.

The Nicaean emperor John III Doukas Vatatzes feared his realm would be the next to fall, but the Mongols showed no interest in expanding. Following the death of Ögedei, the Mongol Empire succumbed to a succession crisis. Apparently, the defeat of the combined Anatolian armies had secured their position and that was enough for them. This also secured Nicaea's eastern border as the Seljuks could no longer credibly threaten the strengthening Nicaean empire.

At the same time, following the death of Bulgarian tsar Ivan Assen II and the devastation the kingdom suffered by the Mongols[13], Bulgaria was mired in succession crises and instability. What used to be the strongest state was now weak and divided. John III exploited the situation and managed to force what used to be the Kingdom of Thessalonica to swear loyalty to him, thus strengthening Nicaea's position in the Aegean. He then proceeded to conquer lands in southern Thrace from both Bulgaria and the Latin Empire (also weakened after the Mongols).

At the same time Michael II Doukas, king of Epirus, used the Bulgarian weakness to take over Albania and parts of Macedonia (the region, not today's country of Northern Macedonia). John III also pushed into Macedonia against Epirus, at one point uniting with a Bulgarian noble and military commander, Dragotas, who switched sides and convinced the local population that it was better to join Nicaea.

Direct conflict between Nicaea and Epirus was avoided but John III turned to the east, helped by Dragotas, and by 1247 all Latin garrisons in Thrace were overrun, the Latin Empire under

---

[13] Bulgaria was hit particularly hard because it ambushed the Mongols on their way towards Ukraine, and so Batu Khan laid such waste north of the Balkan range, that Bulgaria had to agree to become a vassal state to what would later become the Golden Horde.

Baldwin II was completely surrounded, and only held Constantinople. Baldwin II called upon Venice for financial help as he needed coin to pay for reinforcements from Europe (and, in fact, left his son as collateral for repayment). In 1251, Epirus tried to take over Thessaloniki but failed and the skirmish with Nicaea resulted in Epirus losing almost all of Macedonia.

1254 saw the death of John III and the succession of Theodore II Laskaris. About the time when the Polo brothers were arriving in Constantinople in 1255, there were clashes between Bulgaria, who was trying to recover Thracian lands, and Nicaea. The Bulgarian army was soundly defeated but this only strengthened Nicaea's grip on the lands surrounding Constantinople. Theodore's forces were now based in Adrianople, which was the land gateway to the Golden Horn and Nicaea never hid its intentions to take the city back from the Latins. I can't imagine the people living in the city were not the least bit concerned about what may happen on the next day.

With Bulgaria reeling and becoming increasingly decentralized, Theodore II felt Nicaea's position was dominant. He demanded that Michael II Doukas cede the northern reaches of Epirus, so Nicaea could control the entirety of Via Ignatia, which crosses the Balkan Peninsula east-west in what is today northern Greece. Michael II could not overcome Nicaea alone so he joined forces with the Duchy of Morea and the Kingdom of Sicily. Situated on the south of Italy on the other side of the Adriatic, the Kingdom of Sicily had obvious interests in the western Balkan coasts and the strait of Otranto; but just in case, Michael II married his daughter Helena to King Manfred of Sicily, to strengthen the alliance. The clash was inevitable, but Theodore II fell ill and died in 1258. Michael Palaiologos became the regent to the young John IV Laskaris (he got the job after killing the regent that was appointed by Theodore II). Michael then hurriedly sent his brother John Palaiologos west as he expected that Sicilian support would arrive soon in Epirus. John Palaiologos, who had an army assembled in Thessaloniki under the leadership of General Alexios Stratigopoulos marched west but as they were lacking in numbers, they tried to recruit every unit they found available.

The battle of Pelagonia deserves a whole book itself. The armies standing against each other included people of every major nation in the region as well as outsiders (notably, 400 Italian knights from the Kingdom of Sicily fighting for Epirus and 300 German knights, fighting for Nicaea). Once Michael II Doukas met his Morean allies in Pelagonia, John Palaiologos' hurriedly assembled forces were heavily outnumbered. Apart from the Sicilian knights, on the Epirote side, there were 8,000 horsemen and 18,000 lightly armed soldiers; Morea had brought troops from other smaller duchies like Athens and the Archipelago totalling 8,000 heavily armed knights and 12,000 lightly armed troops[14]. On the Nicaean side, apart from native Greek forces, there were Hungarian, Bulgarian, Serbian, Seljuk and Cuman mercenary horsemen and mounted archers; precise numbers are unclear but by a rough estimate, they were outnumbered at least five-to-one, so they had to resort to clever tactics using the agile Cuman riders to harass the heavily armed knights of the

---

[14] These numbers are considered exaggerated by contemporary historians.

opposition, destroying supply wagons and foiling watering for the horses in the difficult mountainous terrain.

John's greatest feat, however, was infiltrating agents within the enemy's camps. This was a complex and recent alliance of interest, so the parties to it hardly trusted each other. His spies spread rumors about desertion and disrespectful behind-your-back talking between commanders. They also obtained information about battle plans. A large Epirote contingent of forces switched sides due to insult by the Frankish knights of Morea, and another left the battlefield, after which, with the knowledge for their battle plans, John managed to surround the Morean army and capture its leader, making Nicaea the undisputed dominant force in the region. After the victory of the battle of Pelagonia, it was already common knowledge that Nicaea would finally come for the prize: Constantinople.

# CHAPTER V
# A FAMILY REUNITED

## Niccolo and Maffeo's Venture

The Polo brothers also had very little doubt in the outcome. They had lived there for years and were familiar with the capabilities of the defenders. The Latin Empire was so greatly outmatched that there was precious little doubt, the city would fall. To the best of my knowledge, there is no evidence of blockades or the likes in the Aegean Sea, but given the ease with which the Nicaeans were moving between Nicaea and Thrace, we can surmise that their fleet dominated that sea and that the Polos knew that a journey back home would be risky. Nicaea did not hide its attitude towards the Latins. On the other hand, Soldaia, the Crimean trading outpost of Venice, offered a relatively safe voyage and interesting potential opportunities. There is little doubt that the Polos understood it was risky staying in Constantinople after the outcome of the battle of Pelagonia made Nicaea dominant in the region. It is also clear that after several years spent in Constantinople, they would have talked to people coming from Crimea and were well aware about the power of the Mongols in general and the Golden Horde in particular. 40 years prior, General Subutai had declared that the Venetians would be the only ones with the right to trade in Crimea and now the Mongols ruled the land. The Polo brothers understood that they needed to travel light, so they turned all the capital they had into valuable jewels and set out to Crimea (they did trade in silk and spices as well, which were premium products but it is obvious that the value added relative to weight and size is greater in jewelry).

Back then, Crimea was still a frontier outpost, the Byzantine Empire controlled a relatively secure location where trade could be made between the steppe nomads and the settled empires of the south. The nomads could traverse the steppes and the rivers with their goods but did not have the means to travel the Black Sea and reach richer lands; moving uninsured bulk cargo over land through hostile and volatile territories was a non-starter. Before the Fourth Crusade, the Black Sea was a domain of the Byzantine Empire as it controlled the Straits. The Bulls issued to Venice, Pisa, and Genoa by Byzantine emperors did not grant them entry into the Black Sea. Trade there primarily served to supply grain, salt, and fish (and slaves). The Latin Empire opened the Straits to Venice but even then, there is little evidence that there was much interest by merchants from Venice in the Black Sea. Trade in the Black Sea remained the domain of the Greeks and the Seljuks, but the Venetians in Constantinople profited from being the intermediaries between the two trade networks at Constantinople. The arrival of the Mongols on the Black Sea's northern shores changed the landscape completely. Crimea was no longer at the forefront of a chaotic domain of warring barbaric horse tribes, it was at the western terminus of Pax Mongolica. The Mongols had retained their interest in trading with the Latins, so Crimea could potentially serve as the point where the two trading networks united. This was no doubt on the mind of the Polos when they left for Crimea.

Still, when we talk about the trading post of Soldaia, one shouldn't imagine a fledgling market city but rather a commodity trading frontier townlet. As already described, the Silk Road(s) represented a series of trade stations where merchants would exchange their goods. Few merchants would travel the entire route but rather a small section of it, where they would sell their merchandise in a relatively safe and familiar environment, often to people they did business with regularly. This meant that a mark-up was added to the price of the goods each time they changed hands and continued their journey east or west. Given the harsh and often dangerous conditions of the road as well as the cost of carrying cargo over land, the mark-ups would have been considerable; so whoever could cut the middle men stood to make great profits while being able to set competitive prices. Soldaia was quickly becoming such a post when the Polos arrived, but it was also attracting droves of other Venetians. And developments in Constantinople were far from favorable for them.

Constantinople was captured in 1261 by the Nicaean Empire, and most of it was razed and burned to the ground, re-establishing The Byzantine Empire. It was of course a bloody and brutal affair, with Latin residents (mercifully) blinded as a punishment for their presence. Those that escaped were either captured again or

68

drowned in boats at sea as they attempted to flee. At this point, Venice lost all of its trading rights in the Black Sea. Michael Palaiologos had enlisted the help of the Genoese navy in the capture of Constantinople but it was never really needed as Baldwin II simply fled the city leaving it wide open to the Nicaeans. Nevertheless, Michael Palaiologos needed somebody to replace the Venetians and their rival Genoa seemed primed for the job. Venice and Genoa had been in open (though low intensity) conflict since 1256 that started over control of Acre in the Holy Land. Venice clearly had the upper hand in the conflict but now they were about to be pushed out of Constantinople and the Genoese would receive a number of trading posts in the Aegean and Black seas, including Soldaia. The alliance between Michael Palaiologos and the Republic of Genoa was shaky from the start and did not last very long. By 1268, Venice had signed a new agreement with Constantinople and had restored much of its previous positions (though now it had to compete with Genoa, which remained the dominant force in the Black Sea). Nevertheless, the Polos could not have known that this would come to pass, certainly not after the savage way their compatriots were treated at the fall of Constantinople. Being blinded was better than being executed but keeping your eyes was better still.

So they left for Sarai Batu, which at the time was already renamed to Sarai Berke, since Batu Khan had recently died and the Golden Horde was now commanded by his brother Berke. Sarai Berke, despite being described as a city, was effectively a combination of two rather large encampments, but with the added benefit of it hosting the ruler of the Golden Horde, Berke Khan. The brothers were welcomed with great honor as few

69

Latins dared to venture into the Steppe and the Mongols were interested in trade with the Venetians and the West. The Polos, apparently familiar with Mongol customs, gave the Khan the jewels they brought as gifts. In return, according to Marco Polo, he gave them "goods worth at least twice their value." He also helped them reach places where they could sell their goods and rake in excellent profits. Apart from that, the first-hand knowledge they gained was invaluable back then: the routes, the terrain, the local habits and tastes, what people sought for and fought over, how much they would pay for it, their wealth, their values, the way they negotiated and did business, and so on.

In the end, the Polo brothers became entrusted trading partners to the khan himself, or what was called back then ortoq merchants (individuals partnered with the state[15]). As mentioned, at the time the Sarai was but a large bivouac and, having spent the good part of the year in it, the Polos ventured further east. This coincides with the time when the Golden Horde attacked Hulagu south into the Ilkhanate, meaning most men of importance would have left the capital to fight. Trying to avoid being caught in another war and with Constantinople still unsafe for Venetians, the Polos traveled east to the Chagatai Khanate, making a 17-day desert crossing and occasionally meeting tartar nomads that were camping in their tents. These were lands they had never seen; landscapes, animals, peoples and habits they had only heard of. They eventually reached Bukhara, where they stayed on for another three years. The city had somewhat recovered from Genghis Khan's conquest three decades prior and was again a

---

[15] We call them cronies today but back then it was not something immoral, since things worked differently.

vibrant market, filled with Chinese Han and Mongol Khitan[16] administrators imposed by the Mongol Empire. This was another interesting practice of the Mongols who would bring Muslim administrators into China and Chinese administrators into Central Asia in order to curtail local people's power.

The brothers describe Bukhara as the finest city in all of Persia, "large and splendid," but the reality is that they were stuck there by the Toluid wars. Bukhara was arguably the safest place to be at the time: to the west, in the Caucasus, Hulagu was retaliating to Berke's raids and to the east Kublai was making a move on Ariq in Mongolia, while quelling a Chinese rebellion. It was an envoy traveling from the Ilkhanate towards China that ended their stay. No Latins were ever seen in Bukhara, so he offered to take them to the Great Khan, who according to him had never seen their like, but was eager to see and get to know more of them and their lands. Kublai Khan was known for his curiosity of foreign peoples and cultures as well as his general thirst for knowledge.

The trip east took a year but when they finally reached Khanbaliq, Kublai, having just been proclaimed as the Great Khan, met them with grandeur, delight and lavish festivities in their honor. He asked them a great deal about the western kingdoms and empires, laws and administration, customs and beliefs, societies, economies, militaries and religion. He took a keen interest in the Pope and the Roman Church. In the end, Kublai decided to send emissaries to the Pope and asked the

---

[16] A nomadic proto-Mongol ethnicity from the Far East.

brothers to act as his envoys along with one of his barons, called Koeketei.

He also gave them a letter requesting at least one hundred educated Christians to be sent to him, who could teach his people Western customs and introduce Christianity to the Empire as well as oil from the Holy Sepulchre. The brothers were given a golden paiza, or gerege, which was basically a golden tablet one foot long and three inches wide. It gave the carrier the ability to acquire lodgings, food and horses throughout the kingdom of Kublai Khan. It also gave them the respect and protection needed from whoever they encountered on what was predictably a perilous journey.

The envoy Koeketei didn't complete the mission, for reasons that have not survived history, but the Polos continued their journey. They were often held by bad weather, mountain passes closed off by snow and flooded riverbeds but eventually, after nearly three years, they reached Ayas on the Levantine coast. From there they went on to Acre in the Kingdom of Jerusalem, in 1269. Here they discovered that Pope Clement IV had died and Christianity in the Levant was under siege. After defeating the Mongol army in 1260, Baibars had begun a protracted attack on the Christian strongholds: Nazareth, Arsuf, Atlit, Haifa, Safed all fell one by one to Baibars's Mamluks until in 1268 he captured Antioch itself; and then continued with Jaffa, Ascalon, Caesarea and Galilee. After the fall of Antioch and before his untimely death, Pope Clement IV called for what would become the ninth and last crusade, led by Edward Longshanks, soon to become king of England.

The Polos met with Theobaldo Visconti (a.k.a. Theobald of Piacenza) in Acre, a legate of the Roman Church, and informed him of Kublai's letter but, seeing this as a great potential win for the church he advised they should wait until a new pope is elected. While Acre was under siege and hostility between Muslims and Christians was high, the Venetians could travel freely because they were instrumental for all parties along with the Genoese. They traded heavily with the Mamluks, especially providing them with metal and timber, which they needed for their armies. So the Polos had no trouble returning to Venice in 1269, with the intention of then delivering the message once the new pope was officially named. They did not know that this pope's election was to drag two years and nine months and become the longest election in the Catholic Church's history (to this date, not just in their time).

In Venice, they met Marco for the first time. One can only imagine Niccolo's feelings meeting his son, who was now fifteen years of age. Venice had changed dramatically in their time away and Marco himself seemed to be an intelligent young man, who clearly had the talent for trading too. He had lost his mother at the age of five (much to Niccolo's distress) and had learnt to read, write, calculate, handle cargo ships, handle foreign currencies, appraise stock, and speak a few languages. It was inevitable that he would now join them on their future journeys. It was here that the great traveler started his small steps to legendary status.

# A Family Trip Begins

The two brothers left with Marco, who was already 17, on a journey back east. Having spent two years idle in Venice, without any sign of a Pope being elected, and knowing how long it would take to reach back to the Khan, they decided they could not wait any longer and set out from Venice to Acre. There, they obtained permission from Theobald of Piacenza to go to Jerusalem and take some of the oil from Christ's sepulcher as promised to the Khan. The legate composed letters to Kublai, where he testified to the brothers' efforts and explained that unfortunately there was yet no pope elected, so they could not comply with the request of 100 monks and the Polos set out on their journey. Around this time, Edward Longshanks arrived crusading in Acre and Theobald joined his efforts. Meanwhile, back in Viterbo, Italy, the College of Cardinals was equally divided between Italian and French cardinals and kept procrastinating the pope's election. The citizens of Viterbo had them locked in the Episcopal Palace, so the cardinals could be pressed hard enough with this important matter and finish the job; this impasse was actually how the tradition with black and white smoke that we witness to this day started. The cardinals tried hard but eventually in August 1271, seeing that the deadlock wouldn't come apart, they decided to elect somebody outside their ranks and the choice fell upon none other but Theobaldo Visconti (Theobald of Piacenza) who, much to his surprise, became Pope Gregory X on September 1st 1271 while warring.

The Polos had just reached Ayas in the Armenian Kingdom of Cilicia when the newly elected Pope sent an envoy and asked them back in Acre; and come back they did on a galley especially sent for them by the king of Armenia. Having been involved in the actual fight against the Mamluks alongside Edward Longshanks who managed to break off the siege of Acre in the summer of 1271, Pope Gregory X sent new letters to Kublai suggesting a military alliance and asking for the mighty Khan's help. By this time however Kublai was pretty busy conquering Song territory and establishing the Yuan dynasty and had limited interest in military campaigns this far west. It was not well understood at the time that China was far more technologically, economically and culturally advanced as well as way bigger than anything European. So to Kublai, Europe and Christianity was a backwater; interesting and intriguing but a backwater. Now, Pope Gregory X perhaps perceived all the Eurasian landmass bar India as Pax Mongolica but in fact, the Golden Horde, the Chagatai Khanate and India all lay between the Yuan dynasty and the Ilkhanate, and they were all hostile to the courts in Khanbaliq and Tabriz. All told, a meaningful alliance between Pope Gregory X and Kublai Khan would have been a tad complicated logistically as it would have required retaking either Central Asia or Russia, while warring with the mighty Songs. No pressure!

The Polos were received back in Acre with graciousness, but then very quickly left for Mongolia, accompanied by two of the best educated Dominican friars in the province: Niccolo de Vicence and Guillame de Tripoli. They were granted privileges by the Pope to ordain priests and bishops and to grant absolution with the apparent idea to enlarge the legation along the way rather than source and send 100 friars outright. It was a hurriedly assembled affair as the Pope was actually still warring and had little time to spare.

Sadly, history hasn't been kind to the friars as it was reported that neither fulfilled the journey due to fear of impending battles, but the Polos, unperturbed, did continue. There were skirmishes between the Armenians and the Mamluks and the monks had little taste for battle, so they abandoned the trek. Cilician Armenia was an ally of the Mongols at the time when Hulagu took Baghdad and Damascus. The Armenians gladly expanded their domain at the expense of the Ayyubid Caliphate but Baibars crushed them in 1266 and took all the lands back, killing masses. Warfare continued as the Armenian Kingdom was not yet broken, but in 1268 a devastating earthquake struck, and by 1269, the Armenian Kingdom of Cilicia had begun paying annual tributes to the Mamluks. Even so, they carried on regular raids and massacres of Christians.

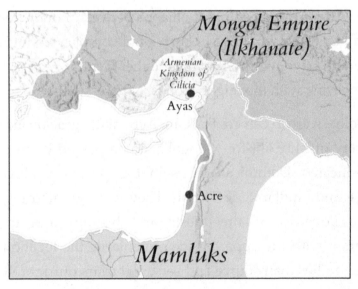

*The Levant*

In Ayas, Marco Polo describes the kingdom as "lesser" Armenia with an atmosphere of decay and decadence, despite its rich lands and its rich vibrant port, where cloths and spices were traded. The nobles, he stipulates, are only good (but then very good) at getting drunk. They didn't spend much time in Ayas as they planned to reach Khanbaliq as soon as possible. Having experienced the land trip across Eurasia and (as Venetian merchants) being experienced sailors, their plan was to board a ship in Hormuz and sail to China.

The Mamluk danger was real, though, and taking the Silk Road to Palmyra through the lands controlled by the Mamluks was not an option. So they set out northeast through the rugged mountainous terrain of Anatolia, where they met with and talked to numerous "rough and uneducated" Turkmen herders who lived alongside astute and educated Greek and Armenian traders and craftsmen. Then through "greater" Armenia, which at the time spanned eastern Anatolia, and was apparently home of the "best buckram[17]" weavers. Marco Polo narrates of the Ark of Noah that can be found in Armenia, sitting "atop of a very high mountain, shaped like a cup" (meaning Mount Ararat, which was not yet climbed at the time). Then he describes how on the Armenian border with Georgia, there is an oil spring that gushes oil at such a speed that a hundred ships can load at once. It is fascinating to consider how young Polo's merchant instinct saw value wasted at a great rate at the site of that spring. At a time when Europe was heating itself only with wood, as coal was yet unknown, oil was the only thing the locals burned. It's

---

[17] A stiff cotton cloth with a loose weave.

not good to eat, he narrates, but is good for salving scabies and it burns pretty well. Little did he know!

Marco Polo proceeds to describe Georgia, although it was not on their route and it is not clear the Polos visited the Georgian Kingdom at all. It wouldn't have been an easy trip. In fact, one of the main things he describes is the narrow and dangerous mountain pass that separates Georgia from what he called "greater" Armenia and which kept Alexander the Great himself away from Georgia (though apparently not Subutai or Hulagu). He also says the Georgians weave the most gorgeous cloths of silk and gold, so one can speculate they may have detoured for merchandise.

# CHAPTER VI
# PERSIA

## Persian Travails

The Polos eventually arrived in the capital of the Ilkhanate Tabriz (which was actually pronounced Tauris at the time). The city left a great impression on Marco Polo, though he was not impressed by the citizens. I will reprint a quote from the 'Travels of Marco Polo' here to both relate his experience with Tabriz and give you a sense of the actual book.

> "Tauris is a great and noble city, situated in a great province called YRAC, in which are many other towns and villages. But as Tauris is the most noble, I will tell you about it. The men of Tauris get their living by trade and handicrafts, for they weave many kinds of beautiful and valuable stuffs of silk and gold. The city has such a good position that merchandize is brought thither from India, Baghdad, Mosul and Hormuz, and many other regions; and that attracts many Latin merchants, especially Genoese, to buy goods and transact other business there; the more as it is also a great market for precious stones and pearls. It is a city in fact where traveling merchants make large profits.

*The people of the place are themselves poor creatures; and are a great medley of different classes. There are Armenians, Nestorians, Jacobites, Georgians, Persians, and finally the natives of the city themselves, who are worshippers of Mahommet. These last are a very evil generation; they are known as TAURIZI. The city is all girt round with charming gardens, full of many varieties of large and excellent fruits.*

*The Saracens of Tabriz are wicked and treacherous. For the law that the Prophet Muhammad gave them lays down that they can do as much harm as they like to anyone who does not share their faith, and steal as much as they can from them, without falling into sin, and for this reason they would be great wrongdoers if it were not for the government. And all the other Saracens in the world comport themselves in the same manner."*

This is the way Marco Polo describes throughout his book most places he visited: how the locals make their living, what is traded in the markets, what the locals are like, their religion (Saracens always portrayed as vile creatures); often he would describe what the food is like: fruit, grains, game and wine (which is somehow always pretty good). It is important to note here how back in the 13th century, "Saracens" considered it morally justified to harm people of other faiths, something I very much doubt their actual religion preached, but is known to have been the case. Then again, it was a time of crusades and holy wars when the Christians would joyfully mass slaughter and burn a Muslim city to the ground with the Pope's blessing (and be excommunicated for doing the same to a Christian port). The lands of Muslims and Christians were vast, their populations were constantly interacting and warring, and religion was everything; people were practically brainwashed to convert or kill. So Marco's disdain for Muslims is prevalent throughout the book and not so evident when it comes to Buddhists or Tengrists; he dismisses these as "idolaters" much like a father would dismiss some silly fantasy of a promising child.

He was a bit more charitable when he discussed the monks who lived in the monastery Venerable St. Barsaumo. This beautiful structure had only been built for around a century at the time, but even today is captivating for tourists and visitors. What seemed to attract Polo though was the monks' wearing of a habit that had similarities to the Carmelites. The monks also wore a golden girdle that they placed at the altar of St. Barsaumo, but would use it as well for a gift occasionally, giving it to travelers to help relieve any pain they may have experienced in their bodies.

As for Tabriz, he seemed to see it in two ways. The positive was that it was wealthy and ambitious for success, trade was extensive, and the people were benefiting from it, but the negative was that he genuinely did not appear to like too many of the inhabitants. Still, this was the first major non-Christian city he ever visited, so I guess the unfamiliar environment must have had a stronger impact on him. We can all identify with such feelings at times!

The Polos proceeded through Persia due south and Marco provides an excellent account of the "province." Saveh, the town from where the three Magi were sent to Jesus Christ carrying gold, frankincense, and myrrh. Kala Atashparastan, the town of fire worshipers, three days further: where they worship fire that struck from heaven. After bringing the three gifts to Christ, the

81

kings who bore them returned with a gift from Him, a closed casket; but when they discovered it was just a stone, they threw it into a well as they did not know what to do with it. Fire struck the well from heaven because the stone was given to them to remind them that their faith should be as firm and as steady as the stone. From then on, they carried the fire to the churches in their country and to that day they worshiped it as God. Yazd, a bustling trading center where the silk fabric yazdi is produced. Kerman, where the turquoise stones are mined and produced and where skilled craftsmen make equipment for mounted soldiers: saddles, spurs, bridles, swords, bows, arrows, quivers, or armor, and craftswomen produce fine embroidery embossed in curtains, quilts, pillows, and cushions. Kamadan, the town secluded in an incredibly hot plain to which one would descend for two full days and will find bewildering animals, birds and fruits that cannot be grown in the colder climate of Europe.

He describes Persia as a place of past greatness, now smashed by the Mongols but admits that had it not been for the Mongols, they would have never been able to travel in safety. For the land was full of brutal and bloodthirsty bandits and the Saracens could, according to the laws of their prophet, do as much harm as they could to people of other faiths. This is the main reason why they traveled from Ayas through the mountains of Turkey and Armenia, that were at the time controlled by the Mongols as opposed to the flatlands of Syria that were at the time controlled by Baibars's Mamluks. Throughout Persia they enjoyed the land's riches in various fruits and game and they observed the beautiful horses, bewildering oxen, gargantuan sheep and sturdy donkeys (the latter fetching good profits when shipped all the way to India).

Marco Polo also describes the Qara'unas, a race he claims was of descendants of Mongol fathers and Indian mothers (qara means black in Mongolian). Notorious bandits that roam the high plateaus of Persia and Afghanistan, know the lands like the back of their hands and rob villages by using "diabolical spells that turn the light to darkness" (perhaps in reality, using sandstorms as cover). The fact was that the Qara'unas were founded as a tribe after the battle of Ain Jalut, where the Mongols were crushed by Baibars. When Hulagu returned to the Ilkhanate, his wrath was so great at the defeat that soldiers ran in droves to the Golden Horde in the Caucasus, the Mamluks in Egypt or the southern Chagatai Khanate in Afghanistan, where he could not chase them; the Mongols that fled into Afghanistan gave birth to the Qara'unas (also called Neguderis after their king) in 1262. It is disputed whether the Polos survived an attack by the Qara'unas or whether this was made up by Rustichello da Pisa; in any case it is barely mentioned in the book so if it were true, then Marco was strangely vague about it, despite "many of his companions" being captured or killed.

After riding for five days on the incredibly hot plain of Kamadan, they reached another dangerous slope that descended sharply and the road they used, narrow and treacherous, serpented down for at least 20 miles, after which they entered the plain of Hormuz.

It's also interesting to read about his views on the Persian strait of Hormuz. This again was a huge trading city, that had the benefit of a large port where merchants could arrive by the sea, but that actually was his first criticism. The dhows that were regularly used, did not appear to be too stable for the Polos' taste, and so, instead of traveling along the peninsular as most would, they decided to continue their travels across the land. Marco described the wooden configuration of the vessels in critical terms and suggested that most traders who used such a boat would struggle to survive in the notorious winds that the region suffered from. A key weakness was the fact there was no iron to be found locally, so instead of using nails, they stitched the hulls together with coconut husk threads and then they were greased with fish oil as opposed to waterproof-sealed with pitch as were the European ships. Among other weaknesses, the dhows had only one mast, one sail, one rudder and no deck, which meant that the cargo was kept in the open covered only with skins, while the horses were put on top of it. It is well known that the dhows were only suitable for coastal navigation and even then they were not entirely safe, despite the better predictability of the Indian Ocean's winds and currents. And it is no surprise that the Venetians, accustomed to top class ships and sailing conditions in the Mediterranean, were horrified at the mere sight of the dhows and the idea of sailing days, let alone weeks in one.

The local climate, as Marco Polo describes it, was particularly difficult for those who were not used to the very high temperatures, and the strong winds that afflicted the city regularly. Summers were so hot that the locals were leaving the city and spent them at higher elevations in their gardens, where they would use the rivers and lakes to escape from the hot desert wind. All the crops and fruit were grown in the winter months from November till the end of March. There were stories (probably exaggerated) of kings who wanted to capture the city with thousands of soldiers, only for the attack to be thwarted by the heat and the wind. The stories kept the city safe it seems. Under King Ruknuddin Ahmad, the people felt secure, and the kingdom appeared peaceful.

Across the gulf, there was the town of Qalhat, situated in modern-day Oman, nowadays 140 km south of its capital Muscat and just at the entrance of the Gulf of Oman. It was a very convenient port, a vibrant market and a splendid though heavily fortified city to which the malik of Hormuz would take refuge when confronted by powerful neighbors along the Iranian shore. From there he would command the entire gulf with a relatively small fleet and be able to cut off the entire Persian trade; because taking over Qalhat by land would require taking over all of the eastern Arabian peninsula. The malik of Hormuz would often take advantage of this powerful position to exert influence over neighboring provinces or refuse to pay taxes if and when raised because inevitably the losses from tax collection were far inferior to the losses inflicted when trade in Hormuz stopped.

Like Tabriz, Hormuz was an important trading center, where merchants brought items such as pearls, silk, golden fabrics, precious stones, spices, elephant tusks, gold and artifacts from India. Marco did not enjoy the food, which consisted mostly of salted fish, nuts, dates and onions; he also describes the locals (many of them black-skinned) in a derogatory way, mainly due to the fact that (again) they were Muslim. He was also bemused by the fact that the people mourned a dead relative for up to four years, something which seemed to be unique to the area. He did appreciate the local wine though, which he describes was made of dates and spices and when men not accustomed to it drank it, it purged their bowels violently.

The lack of a proper ship, the horrid climate and the unsavory food drove the Polos back to the province of Kerman into the mainland but they took a different route, to the northeast. The elevated plain was rich in fruit and game and filled with hot baths where the water cured many diseases. The hot mineral water springs which fed these baths were also running below ground and was the main source for irrigation; its bitterness would pass into the wheat, so the bread produced in this province was so bitter that only the locals could put up with it.

Then the plain turned into a great salt desert (which is in the middle of modern-day Iran) where one could find no food or water for days on end. The Polos traveled through this desert for a week before finally reaching the town of Kuhbanan, where unlike in Hormuz, iron and steel were abundant. Marco Polo adds "ondanique" to the duo, likely referring to the expensive and secretive Indian steel (nowadays known as Wootz steel), which was used for the making of the sharpest and toughest sabres at the time. The technology of production of Indian steel was well guarded at the time but Marco Polo witnessed another local production process: that of tutty, which was produced from the unique local earth. The locals would put the special earth in blazing furnaces with an iron grating on top of it; the vapor given off by the earth would stick to the grating, thus forming the tutty and when scrubbed off would be exported as salve for the eyes and ointment for the skin. The residue in the furnace would be sold or used as spodium (also with medical purposes). It is interesting to note that this town was situated in the middle of nowhere, as Marco describes that upon leaving it, they traveled for another week across uninhabitable desert.

After this eight-day trek through arid lands with no trees or drinkable water, they reached Tun-Qaen, the last of the eight provinces of Persia and the gateway to Central Asia. Marco Polo provides a description of the plain with the Solitary Tree, called the Dry Tree by Christians: a tree that stood alone within a hundred-mile radius. The locals would claim this was the battlefield where Alexander the Great fought Darius III; he describes the locals as Muslims and as handsome people (especially the women who "are inestimably beautiful"), which is perhaps the first time he says anything positive about Muslims. I guess the right pair of (ahem) eyes often puts things in perspective, especially for young men.

## Assassins Creed

If there is one segment of Marco Polo's book that causes more controversy than any other, it is probably his description of the Old Man of the Mountain. And his assassins. The popular video game Assassin's Creed (and the attendant Hollywood movie) was inspired by this precise community. This was a group whose notoriety stretched throughout the centuries, but as with most historical figures that capture our imagination, fact and fiction are often mixed and hardly distinguishable.

It is beyond dispute that the Assassins did exist. The first mention of the group in the West was in 1167, when a Spanish rabbi, Benjamin of Tudela, who was traveling on a 13-year journey through the Middle East and Asia, came across them and chronicled their adventures. It's fair to say that his immediate description of this band of killers provoked horror throughout Europe, and it is this same generational band that Marco Polo described a century later.

They originated in 1090 as a Shia Muslim sect (the Nizari Isma'ili), founded by Hasan-i Sabbah. The sect was not born out of any massive differences in religious beliefs but because of a succession crisis, where it supported Nizar ibn al-Mustansir in the Fatimid Caliphate. That same year they gained prominence after the capture of the castle of Maymun-Diz in the Alamut Valley in northern Iran. The sect started forming a state by a string of fortresses throughout Persia and later Syria and became a great menace to the Abbasid, Fatimid and Seljuk empires. Their castles, situated in hard-to-reach places, were all but impregnable for the conventional forces of the empires. Nevertheless, the Assassins were much weaker than their rivals in terms of military technology and sheer numbers, so they relied on hand-to-hand combat, guerrilla warfare, espionage and tracking down and killing the leaders of the opposing forces to weaken the morale of their soldiers; their preferred methods were arrow(s), dagger or poison.

All told, the Assassins lived mostly in the Persian mountains[18], near the Caspian Sea, and obeyed a leader, or Grand Master, a title handed down throughout the centuries. The Old Man of the Mountain was a nickname given by the crusaders of the Second Crusade and particularly associated with Sheikh Rashid al-Din Sinan, who ruled the sect for nearly 30 years (1169-1193). While the entire Nizari Isma'ili sect is nowadays referred to as "the Assassins," the actual assassins who are the notorious villains that make the story interesting were a small number of selected disciples that were trained and kept at Maymun-Diz, better known today as the Alamut Castle, just south of the Caspian Sea.

It is said that there they lived in a luxurious garden between two high mountains, living off the delicious fruits and herbs that were grown in it. There were beautiful palaces and dwellings, where the inhabitants lived in an almost paradisiacal state. The women were particularly adept at various arts like playing music, singing, dancing and seducing, whereas the men were addicted to hashish. A mispronunciation of the Arabic word hashashun, or hashish-eater, is where the English word 'assassin' eventually came from. They were mostly youths and were given this in such high quantities, that they would be carried to bedrooms where, upon awakening, they were surrounded by the most beautiful damsels who would entertain them. Add to this wine conduits across the garden (also water, milk and honey ones for whoever is interested) and this gave the men the feeling that they were in paradise. Then only complete and total obedience to the Grand Master would enable them to return, so

---

[18] They had perhaps over 50 castles in Persia and only about 15 in Syria.

for them going on a mission, it was a win-win: if they survived, they would return to Alamut, and if they did not, they would go to Paradise, which they figured was about the same or even better.

The Assassins were eventually defeated by the Mongol Empire (who else?) under Hulagu Khan. It is said this happened after unsuccessful attempts by no less than 400 assassins to kill Möngke Khan. He was extending the empire to the west, and in 1256, Hulagu engaged and defeated the hash-binging damsel-loving hitmen by taking their (previously thought of as impregnable) castles one by one. The Mongols were able to take the castles and palaces due to their siege prowess; they had wooden slingshots and Chinese-designed advanced catapults that could throw gunpowder (as well as huge arrows and other projectiles) at enormous distances with power and precision previously unheard of. Sometimes, they would climb a neighboring peak, carrying their huge weapons with them in pieces, re-assemble, and attack from there (that is what they did at Alamut). The Assassins didn't give up easily though, and the long and drawn-out battles have been described down the years in brutal terms.

Victory was finally assured when the leader, Rukn al-Din Khur-Shah, was captured and paraded in front of the walls of every castle. He was then taken to the Mongolian capital, Karakorum, where Möngke Khan refused to see him. He was returned to the mountains but assassinated on the way by being trampled to death by the Mongolian guards. The group then effectively disappeared.

Alamut Castle (also known as the Eagle's Nest) is most likely what Marco Polo describes in his travels, perhaps relating the locals' narrative because the castle (and its famed library) fell to Hulagu in 1256, 15 years prior. Iran's Cultural Heritage Organization develops the site of Alamut Castle today as a tourist attraction. The archaeological work that has been going on since the 1990s has discovered plenty of evidence that Alamut was a robust knowledge center with an observatory, a library and a mosque, which was dug into the solid rock. They have not discovered any evidence of the described gardens (with conduits running with wine, milk, honey and water), nor any hashish plantations. That said, any young fighting man then, now and always, will testify that if there are beautiful, well-disposed women on site, then the beautiful gardens become somewhat less important (with the wine conduit a nice-to-have rather than a must-have and everything else pretty much irrelevant).

# CHAPTER VII
# CENTRAL ASIA

## Pamir Crossing

The Polos' journey continued east through Afghanistan's lush plains, valleys and the occasional desert. They passed through Shebergan, where they found the best melons in the world, which locals would leave in the sun to dry and then they tasted sweeter than honey. Then Balkh at the edge of the Ilkhanate, where Alexander the Great married Darius's daughter and where they saw plenty of marble mansions and palaces, ruined by the Mongol invasion a few decades ago. Then crossing into the Chagatai Khanate and riding twelve days to Taloqan, which had a market with mountains of salt ("the best in the world"), grains, almonds and pistachio. It seems the men Marco Polo describes as Muhammad worshipers were only getting worse the further he traveled to the north east: in modern-day Afghanistan he describes men in balaclavas, dressed only in self-hunted, self-made and self-tanned animal skins, who were "wicked and murderous" and whose favorite occupation was getting drunk on the local ("excellent") boiled wine.

Then crossing briefly into modern-day Tajikistan to Iskashim on the Panj River, where he describes how the locals dug their dwellings into mountain caves and the hunt for porcupines, which would curl in a bowl and shoot their quills at the men and dogs hunting them. He describes the province of Badakhstan (in the extreme north-east of Afghanistan) as a place of narrow passes and natural strongholds that was very cold, difficult to traverse and even more difficult to invade. Yet, it was a place of great riches with an abundance of spinel (balas rubies), lapis lazuli and silver; he was also fascinated by the horses and falcons that were bred there. The people in this secluded province were predominantly Tajik[19] who spoke their own language; their nobles claimed to be the offspring of Alexander the Great and Stateira (daughter of Darius III). This is where the Polos stayed for nearly a year as Marco fell ill by a strange – and he describes it as fatal – illness, which some historians suggest may have been malaria. Having heard that the locals would take to the mountains and the purer air to cure themselves of the illness, his father and uncle persuaded him to do the same, and it is believed that it was Badakhstan's climate that eventually cured him. Alas the book is focused on the places and peoples rather than on Polo's own personal experiences, so there is not much information about his illness in it.

The Polos continued northeast through the Wakhan pass and into Pamir, which Marco Polo describes in his manuscripts as being the 'Highest Place in the World.' This was the first time he would ascend to elevations of such height that even no birds

---

[19] Unlike most Central Asians, the Tajiks are a Persian and not a Turkic tribe.

would be seen flying there. He was overwhelmed by the landscape and the incredible events that took place daily. He referred to a phenomenon as he traveled through Afghanistan as the 'Land of Fire,' and this is something that can still be seen today. For over 4,000 years, there have been fires that spontaneously burn on the surface, fed by the natural gasses that sometimes leak to it. Polo also described them as 'cold fires,' although that appears to be a somewhat inaccurate description of an event that still captivates tourists today. At the time of Marco Polo's experience of the fires, they were plentiful and all of them burned brightly, but nowadays commercial gas extraction has effectively put out most. They once played a very key religious role in the Zoroastrian faith, as fire was regarded as a link between human beings and the supernatural world. East of Baku, there is still the Ateshgah Fire Temple (the word Ateshgah comes from the Persian meaning 'home of fire') which still attracts many visitors today. In Polo's time, this was one of many temples where caravans could stay and rest, plus worship the God of their choice, as fire was supposed to represent all. Today, only one real fire remains burning – the Yanar Dag – but some say that it was only ignited in the 1950s, and it is now fed from Baku's main gas supplies.

The Wakhan pass is the only border crossing between Afghanistan and China but it is such a remote and rugged area that even today there is no modern road made. It is described as a trade route but it is doubtful that the pass is used today even for drug smuggling. In 1906 Sir Aurel Stein, a Hungarian-born British archaeologist who conducted extensive explorations in Central Asia, reported that yearly 100 pony loads of goods would cross into China at the Wakhan pass. If that was true, then few other places would have had trade volumes this low (North and South Poles included). In the 1990's the locals were barely aware that Afghanistan was undergoing a civil war and then had little clue about a 20-year American occupation because nobody bothered to visit the region. The Polos set out to the Far East to trade and not to go sightseeing remote areas so that Marco could write a book, so why did they not go north on the normal Silk Road through the markets of Bukhara and Samarkand, but chose instead to ride through northern Afghanistan, the Wakhan pass and the dangerous Pamir mountains? The short answer to this question is: calculated risk, because in 1272 when they would have made this crossing, the road through Bukhara was more dangerous due to a skirmish between the Chagatai Khanate and the Ilkhanate.

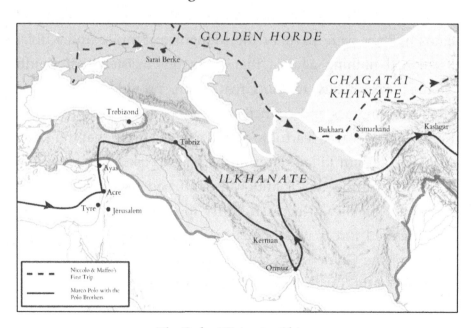

*The Polos' Trips to China*

We ended the story of the Mongol Empire's fragmentation with the deaths of Ariq (Kublai's brother), Hulagu (of the Ilkhanate), Berke (of the Golden Horde), and Alghu (of the Chagatai Khanate) but there is more to the story (in fact, there are two centuries of Eurasian history well worth studying after these events). The successor of Alghu, Mubarak Shah, became the first ruler of the Chagatai Khanate to be converted to Islam, but his rule was short-lived as he was forcibly replaced by the great grandson of Chagatai Khan Ghiyas-ud-din-Baraq (who also converted to Islam). In 1266 the latter came into conflict with Kublai Khan over the Tarim basin (modern-day Xinyang) and, as Kublai was too busy in China, Baraq's forces prevailed. Meanwhile Kaidu, a grandson of Ögedei and leader of the House of Ögedei, figured the time was ripe for him to enter the fray. He felt that Kublai owed him a share of the conquered lands as they were parts of the Mongolian Empire and Kublai Khan had nothing against that claim but insisted that Kaidu should swear fealty to the Great Khan, provide soldiers and attend ceremonies and councils in the palace when summoned. Kaidu however was fearful to attend as he thought that the Khan would have him killed; after all he had accused him of siding with Ariq during the Toluid wars and had had Alghu of the Chagatai Khanate unsuccessfully try to capture him in 1263. So Kaidu joined forces with the successor of Berke Khan, Mengu Temur of the Golden Horde and together they pushed Baraq's army out of the Tarim Basin with overwhelming force and drove them west to Transoxiana.

Now that he had an important piece of the Chagatai Khanate, he had no need to swear fealty to Kublai in any manner and remained a hostile power to the Yuan dynasty's western border. The Netflix series incorrectly placed Kaidu (and Ariq) in the Khan's court when Marco Polo arrived in Khanbaliq. It is more likely that Polo never saw Kaidu or his daughter and his vivid descriptions of her are based on what he had heard from others. She was a real piece of work by the way, strong, sturdy and independent. Her name Ayuruq meant "Shining Moon" in Mongol, but it seems her favorite pastime was making young men see shining stars in broad daylight. There was no man that could overpower her, she would beat up everybody. Kaidu wanted to marry her, but she told him she would only marry a noble who could subdue her in a fight. Kaidu was no fool, so his decision was along the lines of anyone wise who has had the blessing of fathering such a brat (myself included): he figured "ok, what the hell..." So, Shining Moon made it a standing challenge tournament: any young noble was invited to try and marry her. And it didn't sound like much of a challenge, all the man had to do was throw her to the ground before she threw him. Success would mean he got her hand in marriage, failure meant he would part with 100 horses. This is how Ayuruq raised more than 10,000 horses and she never got married. It goes without saying she was also one of the fiercest warriors and her father took her into many battles. I have a hard time imagining how they did those things back then: you can throw yourself into battle without knowing whether you'd make it out alive, but sending your daughter into the fray? I don't know. Anyways, back to the storyline.

In 1267, Baraq accepted peace and relinquished the Tarim basin to Kaidu who gradually became very influential in Chagatai's court.

In 1270 he convinced Baraq to attack Khorasan, a far flung isolated northeastern province of the Ilkhanate, ruled by one of Hulagu's sons, prince Buchin. Baraq's campaign was successful at first but in 1270, the Ilkhan Abaqa came to his brother's aid and defeated Baraq badly. On his way back to Transoxiana Baraq fell from his horse, crippled himself and died the following year, which happened about the time when the Polos set out from Ayas. A succession struggle then broke out and Kaidu successfully pushed aside Baraq's four and Alghu's two sons, imposing Negubei, a protégé of his but in 1272 as the khan. Abaqa used this unstable situation to invade Transoxiana and sack Bukhara. This is the most likely reason why the Polos chose to take the Wakhan pass and climb one of the highest and most dangerous mountains in the world, while Abaqa and Kaidu were warring over Bukhara.

This trek however would place Marco Polo's name in zoology's textbooks (not that he saw any of it). On the plain of Pamir, where according to him was the best pasture in the world, he saw a strange sheep that was "great in size" and had long and large, spiraling horns, sometimes reaching "six palms in length" (this is about 50cm, but species are known to have horns of over 1m in length and the world record is 1.9m). Their horns were so large that the locals used them to make eating bowls and so long that they used them to build fences.

In 1758 Swedish naturalist Carl Linaeus renamed them as 'argali,' a type of sheep that was only found in the mountainous regions of East Asia, the Himalayas, Tibet and the Altai Mountains. Indeed, if you have ever traveled to these places, you will almost certainly have seen this curious looking animal, with its great horns. The spiral continues until the tips of the horns, which are incredibly sharp, face away from the head in a horizontal position. The sheep are universally coloured brown, with a white underbody, and apparently, they have a lifespan of around 12 to 13 years. There have been stories of American hunters in particular, paying in the region of $40,000 to shoot and capture one of the sheep, and for that reason, a National Reserve has been set up to protect them. The Khunjerab National Park and the Parmir Peace Park have both attempted to set borders to protect the animals, but it is a costly, and sometimes, thankless task.

The Polos spent nearly two months crossing the Pamir mountains, traveling at great elevations through uninhabited areas and inhospitable conditions. It takes a stretch of the imagination to think of the dangers they must have been facing every day – walking narrow paths that hung over steep slopes, sleeping rough in sub-zero temperatures, encountering wild animals. What scarce people they met were, by Marco Polo's account, idolaters, complete savages, and "mightily bad people."

The Polos had the paiza, or Golden Passport, as they were later named, which afforded them safety, lodgings, food and horses. They weren't a guarantee though, and in the vast, near impossible to police wilderness that was Pamir, it was inevitable that bandits would attack travelers and those moving in caravans, sometimes putting the travelers to death. One such attack took place against the Polos on their way to Kashgar; unfortunately, there is little information about it. The narrative is that the three Polos fought ferociously and managed to evade capture, but in a Mongol State that actually promoted a type of law and order, this was a relatively isolated incident.

In any case, they overcame Pamir and descended into China at the province of Kashgar. I include here a direct quote from the book (obviously translated into an easy-to-understand English) that describes both a type of an encounter with strange men they met in the mountains, Marco's growing curiosity about Kublai Khan, the city and market of Kashgar, and the seriousness with which his experienced father and uncle approached crossing the Taklamakan and Gobi deserts:

> "'These men looked tired and overworked, with a strong odor that seemed to linger. The three small, yet loud men were on their way, proceeding down the mountains just as we made it up. We continued. They continued on as well, but the things they said about the great Khan continued to linger in the back of my mind. Their description, parallel to the constructive talk from my family, had really begun to pique my interest. Still hoping to meet this man, I cannot wait, but for now the open-air market in Kashgar quickly became my savior. The hustle and bustle of this market, with the expensive and valuable goods provided by merchants, and the commodities being provided by the local trade, showed just how big of a deal this trading town was. However, Niccolo and Maffeo were not as enthused by the complexity that entailed. The two were taking all necessary precautions before entering the Taklamakan Desert and receiving what the Gobi would have in store for us. Although they have passed through the Gobi before, it has been many years since, and both of them realized the severe risks associated with doing so."

# Western China and the Taklamakan Desert

Marco Polo describes the northwest provinces of China that skirt the southern reaches of the Taklamakan desert in similar terms: about five days travel through each of Kashgar, Yarkand, Khotan, Pem, and Cherchen (the first two part of the Chagatai Khanate under Kublai's nephew, the rest part of China under Kublai himself). The people worshipped Muhammad and there were Nestorian Christians; living was mostly by trade and crafts; there was an abundance of cotton growing; and there were plenty of farms, orchards, vineyards and ... sand. In Yarkand, he noticed that the locals were extremely prone to a disease called goiter, which causes a lump or swelling on the neck. It was the same affliction that the second of North Korea's leaders – the Supreme Leader, Kim Il-sung - attempted to hide from his people towards the end of the last century. Marco put the problem down to the poor drinking water. In the rivers of the provinces of Pem and Cherchen he also describes an abundance of jade and chalcedony, which were traded to the east in China for great profits. In Pem, when a man left on a journey for more than 20 days, it was customary for the woman to take a temporary replacement husband; the men would also take substitute wives wherever they went. In the book, this convenient arrangement is described in a calm, matter-of-fact way one wouldn't expect from the staunch, morally superior, Saracen-disparaging Christian that Marco was. Cherchen, already in more arid lands, closer to the Taklamakan desert was, according to him, badly ravaged by the Mongols. People there would store their harvest far from their dwellings in hidden sand caves, so that passing armies would not loot it; they would also flee with their livestock in surrounding deserts to wells that only they knew about, so passing armies basically had hard times in these lands.

After Cherchen, they reached the city of Lop at the edge of the Taklamakan desert, which he called "The Great Desert" or "The Desert of Lop." They spent a week in Lop to recuperate and then stocked up a month's worth of supplies, so they could make the crossing. Even today this crossing is quite a challenge as the Taklamakan desert is one of the largest and most inhospitable in the world. Attempting to cross it with modern machinery, technology and satellite navigation would still be a major expedition, yet Marco Polo did this in the 13th century. It's extraordinary to say the least. He managed to cross it via its narrowest route, yet it still took around 30 days to complete. Despite the obvious dangers of such a monumental journey, where virtually no soul was seen, he described it as being a relatively safe travel. The one thing that made the journey possible was that there were water wells dispersed throughout the desert in about 28 places, sufficient to supply a party of a hundred men and their animals. The fact that they did not have to carry a month's worth of water supplies with them was surely a relief.

It was while he was traveling across this huge desert plain that he came across the curiosity of singing sand dunes. This was an extremely concerning moment for him, as he immediately thought that they were brought about by mysterious and evil spirits. That is hardly surprising when you look at it from a 13th century viewpoint; and bearing in mind this phenomenon had never been experienced by anyone outside of the desert, it's entirely understandable. He describes, in a rather matter-of-fact manner, how travelers would hear the spirits talking at night, especially if they somehow remained alone, say if they were left behind or wandered astray of camp. The sounds were sometimes like whispers, sometimes like musical instruments and sometimes even like drums. These sounds could be heard during the day as well but I guess hearing the spirits talking or jamming in the dead of night was a lot more ... well, spooky.

We now know why sand dunes appear to sing to us. At first, it was believed that the dead were banging drums to attract those who walked above. Then, it was suggested that there were underground streams and the water rushing through the tunnels was making the sound, but at the start of this century, it was finally explained. It seems that it is as simple as grains of sand that fall down a high dune, creating an avalanche-type effect. So, if Marco Polo and his father and uncle, plus the caravan that accompanied them, displaced the sand as they trekked, the avalanche would sing out to them. It is of course a little more complex, but inside these dunes there is a layer of hard sand with a layer of soft sand on top of it. It's only when the soft sand tumbles over the hard, that the sound of whistling (mistaken for singing) can be heard. One can only imagine the effect it had on a 13th century traveler, visiting those places where no European had ventured before. It wasn't an evil spirit at all, but rather a sound that can lift a spirit to those tourists who are fortunate enough to experience it today.

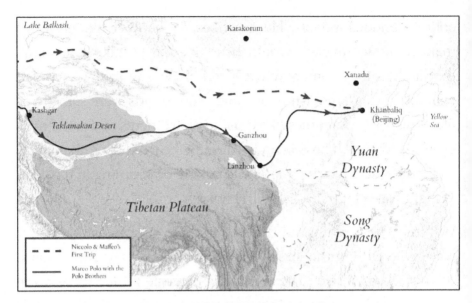

*The Polos' Trips through China*

When the Polos emerged from the Great Desert they entered the city of Shazhou. Here, Polo was amazed by the habits of the "idolaters" when they buried their dead. They would burn them but only on the date that their astrologer said was appropriate, which could be a week, a month or even six months away. During the waiting period, the body would remain in their family home and the family would embalm the body with spices and camphor, wrap it in silk cloths (as silk was abundant in these lands), and place it in a coffin with very thick walls, which was beautifully painted. They would also put food and wine every day for the soul to eat and would prepare paper drawings of horses, camels, slaves, and coins to burn with the body, so that he or she would have them as possessions in the next world (a tradition that the Mongols also adhered to).

Even more amazed was he with the habits in the province of Kumul, which also lay on the verge of the Great Desert (and before a smaller desert that would take three days to cross). The province had plenty to offer in terms of food and beverages and its inhabitants (also idolaters) would live off the fruits of the earth, sell them to travelers and indulge in playing instruments, singing, dancing and ... carnal pleasures. Strangers were welcome to the land and when a stranger approached a house and asked to stay in, the man would leave him with his wife and stay away for two or three days, while the wife pleased the guest, including in bed. This he experienced at a time when women caught in adultery in Europe were whipped, their heads shaven, and paraded on the streets before being enclosed in a monastery for the rest of their lives (unless the cheated husband would have them back); and stoned to death by Sharia law in Islamic lands.

In the city of Ganzhou, where the Polos stayed for a while recuperating and trading, Marco Polo describes usage of their calendar with lunar cycles, Buddhist monasteries with huge "idols" and the customary polygamy where a man could have as many wives as he could support (but the first one would always have the highest status). Ganzhou was just south of the Gobi Desert across which, to the north, lay the old Mongolian capital of Karakoram (a near two-month journey north through nearly uninhabited lands). The Polos spent around a year in these lands and Marco made some excellent observations on the Mongol way of life.

# CHAPTER VIII
# THE LANDS OF THE YUAN

## The Mongols

Marco Polo witnessed how the Mongols of the Steppe lived, moving their camps according to the seasons' requirements for pasture: down to the steppes during the winter and up to the colder mountains and valleys during the summer, when the steps were hot and arid. This was no small feat as they tended to have plenty of animals moving with them: horses, mares, oxen, camels, sheep and goats. They would move with their houses, which consisted of a light and neat wooden construction that could be easily dismantled and then mounted again, and covered with pelts. They could transport these houses, called yurts, on light two-wheeled carts, so well covered with black leather that everything in them stayed dry even with the heaviest of rains. They would travel in these carts, pulled by oxen or camels, with their families, their yurt, food and everything they needed in them, they would reach a place of good pasture and re-assemble their yurts with the door always facing south. Marco noted that the Mongols would eat any meat including game, horses, dogs and even mongooses, which were abundant in the Steppe. He seems to have liked their traditional kumis drink, fermented mare's milk, which according to him resembled white wine. That's not really the case, especially with the lighter sorts of white wine, but then Marco dubbed wine (throughout the book) anything that had alcohol.

The Mongolian horsemen were legendary, even in their contemporary times, and that legend has been carried through to the modern day. Their main weapon was the recurved, composite bow, constructed with bamboo, horn, sinew and animal glue (rendered from connective tissue), which made them lighter to carry, and far more accurate than any other bows at the time. This was combined with two types of arrows: light ones with a small sharp blade made of bone for long range shooting and heavy ones with a broad metal head, toughened in brine and able to pierce armor at close distances; their usual quivers could pack around 60 arrows. It is said they could hit any target up to 250 meters away (twice the range of English longbows), whilst galloping at around 45 mph. This was of course without holding onto the reins of the galloping horse but using their strong thighs to guide it. That in itself, is something quite extraordinary.

When engaging with an enemy, there would be a front row of warriors, with each one of them skilled bowmen. Then the row behind would have fewer bowmen. This was so that if any front row bowman was killed, there would immediately be a replacement, giving the enemy the impression that the army was still as strong and untouched. In the Mongol cavalry, six out of ten horsemen would be light cavalry like the already described

107

mounted archers, while the other four would be heavy cavalry or lancers. The latter would be armed with (of course) lances, often with hook and snare, which was a Mongol innovation, maces and sabres (a.k.a. scimitars).

It was part of a Mongol's teaching and upbringing that they should be able to ride and fight and shoot arrows to perfection by the time they were young adults. This also included women, as they played a far larger part in a Mongol's lifestyle than expected. During peaceful times, the men (who practiced polygamy) would hunt and engage in falconry, whilst the women would take care of domestic duties, but also learn to ride and fight. One thing that impressed Marco Polo during his time with the Mongols, was that the women were as respected as much as the men, even though they were also expected to marry the eldest son of her husband once he died; that excluded first wives as they did not marry their own sons of course.

The Mongolian horsemen were feared greatly throughout the region, mainly because of the brutality they brought to their battles, but sometimes it's easy to forget the role that the foot soldiers played too. It has been said that they were far better and more accurate archers than their mounted compatriots, but this is maybe because they didn't have the added problem of riding a horse at great speeds. Instead, they were some of the most advanced soldiers of their time. They used a thumb ring for shooting, which was normally made of silver, another Mongol innovation, which hadn't been introduced anywhere else. Their talents and abilities included shooting an arrow with and against the wind, shooting whilst walking, and shooting whilst running.

They were also taught how to unstring their bows with their feet, keeping their hands free for any possible hand-to-hand combat. Bow and arrow was their main weapon but they also used halberds, sabres, axes and clubs in close combat.

So, what made them all so successful? As with most cases where warriors became superior to others, it was down to the effective integration of weaponry, which then afforded superior tactics. First, they wore light armor on their bodies, made of tough boiled water-proof buffalo leather (that doubled over their chest for extra protection), along with specially made protective silk undershirts with metallic threads. So whether riding or walking, they were extremely mobile, yet well protected. Their light cavalry could thus adopt tactics that were either dangerous or downright impossible for others. Then they had an also superior composite bow (as already described) that was the most feared weapon on the planet. That was until the advance of gunpowder (which the Mongols, ever looking to adopt new technologies, were the first to use in battle). Finally, it was also down to the power of the horse, for without a strong and fast horse, how could they fight?

The Mongolian horse hasn't changed at all down the centuries. It's said that, even today, the number of them now outnumbers the population. The horses are of a stocky build with short legs, which was an important trait as it allowed them to steer with speed and agility other horses were incapable of; that in turn was a main tenet of the Mongol hit and run tactics whereby upon being chased, the Mongol riders would suddenly make a U-turn, steering the horses with their legs only, and spray the chasers with arrows. They are around 14 to 16 hands high and are perfect for either heavy work, or the opposite in racing each other. They have very long mane and tails, which makes them unique compared to others, but this came about by crossbreeding over a thousand years ago.

Their success was also down to their harsh way of life. A Mongol army would not need to carry supplies with it. The horses were accustomed to live on the pasture while the men, many of whom skilled hunters, would live off the game of the land and the beloved kumis they produced. Each man would have two leather flasks to keep the milk he drank, a pot for cooking meat and a small tent to shelter him from wind and rain when needed. And they could carry on for days without food or water, piercing their horses' veins and drinking their blood to quench their thirst (and for nourishment). They would also have dried milk, which felt like paste and could be mixed with water in their flasks, turning into a syrup while shaken up during the horses' ride.

Large armies would send parties of up to 200 men in the vanguard, the flanks, and the rear as scouts, so that there was no surprise attack to the main force. A Mongol lord would command a force of 100,000 horsemen called a tuq. That force would be split into ten units of 10,000 men called a tumen, and each of these would be split into ten units of 1,000 men, which would be split into units of 100 and then units of ten men. Each commander would thus have to deal with ten officers on the level below him (not always a him but most of the time).

If we have to sum-up, the key traits of the Mongol army were a sufficient number of very disciplined warriors with superb weapons and skills in horsemanship and marksmanship, outstanding mobility, a simple well-understood chain of command, and extremely effective tactical doctrine. This helped them build the second largest land empire the world has ever seen without much geographical advantage (that was very helpful for the British to build the largest empire, which peaked 650 years later); and the Polos became the first Europeans to traverse most of it for the first time.

Proceeding east and southeast from Ganzhou throughout Tangut, Polo describes new marvels that he encountered for the first time. Oxen the size of elephants and with hair "three palms long" that could pull twice as strong as ordinary oxen (likely yacks); pheasants twice as big as the ones found in Europe with tails of seven to ten palms long (likely Reeve's pheasants); musk deer and how musk was extracted to use in perfumes, which he saw for the first time (they basically remove a gland found near the deer's navel); fat men with small noses, black hair and no beards; and women with beautiful white skin, delicate build, very well formed limbs and absolutely no hair except on their heads.

Marco observes that the further east they went, the fewer Nestorian Christians one could find. However upon leaving Tangut province and entering the Cathay provinces, they first passed through the kingdom of Tenduk, which was ruled by Christians and, according to him, descendants of Prester John[20].

---

[20] A legendary Christian presbyter and king that Marco Polo makes constant allusions to in his book, but who never really existed. Legend at the time had it that he ruled over a Christian nation in the Far East, which was split off from the Christian lands in Europe by pagans and Muslims. It was believed his lands formed a Christian exclave in either India, Central Asia, or China; Portuguese sailors later thought all Prester John references related to Ethiopia, until they proven wrong in the 17th century.

People in the province lived by trade (to the east), crafts and agriculture, there was an abundance of lapis lazuli and they produced excellent camel hair camlets and a wide variety of gold and silk cloths. What Marco notes is that there was a class called Argon (or half-castes), which were people born of mixed race and religion. And those people, he recounts, were more handsome, intelligent, and better at business than the others. Continuing on to the east, they reached Chagan Nur, a residence of the Great Khan with beautiful forests and lakes where he could spend days hawking for there was an abundance of wild fowl (and a particularly impressive variety of cranes and pheasants).

## The Khan's Capital

Then, finally, after another three-day journey to the northeast, they reached the Khan's summer residence in Xanadu in 1275. As Polo recounts, they were met with great honor and festivities. In fact, it is said that when Kublai heard news of their approach, he sent couriers to escort them and they rode out to meet them for no less than 40 days. The Khan was very interested in every detail of their journey and accepted their gifts, the oil from the Holy Sepulcher and the letters from the Pope with great gratitude. The Pope's letters were proposing a strategic alliance between Christians and Mongols against the Muslims in the Holy Lands but Kublai Khan was not particularly interested in this; as mentioned, the Pope and most Christians at the time did not seem to realize that the Mongols were not a monolithic force but were already splintered into four different parts and that the Great

Khan's interest was first and foremost in the newly established Yuan dynasty, which was at a prohibitive distance to the east. But he took great interest in young Marco Polo who had learned some Mongolian language during the trip and impressed the Khan with wit, thirst for knowledge, intelligence, and humility. The Polos also gained favor quite quickly by introducing a blueprint of the trebuchet, a weapon the Mongols did not yet have at the time. This helped Kublai Khan conquer the last of the remaining fortresses of the Song, which he had trouble with.

The description of Kublai Khan's palace amazes even today. Made out of marble and various other ornamental stones, its inside walls were covered with gilded pictures and images; surrounded by a 16-mile-long wall within which you could find rivers, lawns and groves teeming with all kinds of stags and roebucks. The Khan kept over 200 gyrfalcons and countless of other smaller falcons within his mews and he would ride his horse throughout the compound with his leopard on the back of the horse and would release the animal to hunt him a stag, which he would then feed to the falcons (puts modern-day cartel bosses in perspective, right?). Polo also describes another castle within the walls, made entirely out of bamboo canes, held together by silk threads, with a varnished waterproof roof and walls gilded inside and decorated with images of birds and animals. This palace was made so it could be moved to whatever location the Khan wanted it to be moved (just pause to imagine the logistics of the exercise in the 13th century).

If that does not seem lavish enough, Marco Polo proceeds to describe the Khan's personal life. Kublai had four wives, each of which was an empress with her own court, with no less than 300 ladies-in-waiting along with an army of eunuchs and servants, approaching a grand total of 10,000 each. He had 22 sons, the eldest of which, named Genghis, was considered the heir to the throne but as he had unfortunately passed away, the throne was set to pass to Genghis's eldest son Temur. These were the sons of his wives. Then, there were another 25 by his concubines, which were selected among the fairest and most handsome the land had to offer, sent to bed with one of his barons' wives who was to make sure, the girl was a virgin and healthy in every aspect, then sent to the Khan's chambers along with another five girls like her, where they would spend three days and three nights granting the Khan's every wish. After that, another batch of six girls would be dispatched for another three days and three nights. Come to think of it, 25 sons seems like a pretty low number, but as Marco Polo notes, all of them were proven skilled warriors and were made great barons. Having read all that, I can't help but scoff whenever I read the phrase "larger-than-life" about anyone that does not support 47 sons (daughters not included), 40,000 staff, and a mobile bamboo castle.

The Khan's court would reside in Xanadu for the hot months of June, July, and August and in the capital of Khanbaliq (Beijing) in the winter months of December, January, and February. As Marco Polo recalls, in March, after the winter months had passed, the Khan would head south towards the Ocean Sea[21] for a great hunt of seabirds with no less than 10,000 falconers, which made for a spectacular hunting party, covering a vast area of the

---

[21] Marco seems to call all seas to the east "the Ocean Sea" since they were not yet well known to Europeans.

coast. An even more spectacular view was the Khan himself: sitting atop four specially trained elephants in his cabin, which was lined inside with golden cloth and outside with tiger skins[22], with 12 gyrfalcons to hunt and a few barons to keep him company. After the hunt, they would proceed south to a place called Cachar Modun, where the Khan's huge pavilion covered in and out with the most luxurious pelts would already await amidst thousands of other pavilions, including his guards', sons', and concubines'.

In Khanbaliq, Marco saw what he described as the grandest and most luxurious palace anywhere in the world. It was enclosed all around by a great wall, each of its four sides approximately a mile in length and then there was another wall surrounding it within. Both walls were similar to each other, with the main gates facing south (just like a Mongol yurt would); there were five gates, of which the central one, much bigger than the rest, was never opened, except for the Great Khan when he would leave and return. There were eight armories on either wall – four in the middle of each wall and four at each corner, so a total of sixteen where the war harness was kept. This included horses, bridles, weapons and virtually any type of military equipment that was needed to fight a war. Each armory, a palace itself, housed several hundred soldiers.

The palace had no upper floors but the hall dazzled with the height of its ceiling, the beautiful gold and silver decorations and its vastness. It could easily take 6000 men to sit and dine in it. There were so many rooms that led off from the main hall, that

---

[22] Marco Polo calls them lion skins but describes them to have black, white, and orange stripes.

Polo wrote that the building was so rich and so beautiful, that no man on earth would be able to build anything quite like it. Kublai Khan's private rooms, where only his concubines were allowed to enter, were full of his treasures of gold, silver and gems, plus gold plated walls and ceilings. And of course, there was a park, where one could find a variety of deer and other animals, along with a lake full of fish. There was also a hill, known as the Green Hill, that overlooked the palace gardens, which had been especially constructed, seeded with the greenest grass and covered with green lapis lazuli; and there the Khan had the finest trees, uprooted and imported from around the world, and re-planted for him to enjoy. It was the most magnificent building to be found anywhere in Asia, and quite possibly anywhere on earth. And because one is rarely enough, the Khan had an exact copy of his palace built on the opposite side of a man-made lake (wall, armories, park, etc.), connected by a bridge, where his grandson Temur would reside in preparation to take his place.

The Palace of the Sheng (or superior court) was also found in Khanbaliq. The Sheng consisted of the 12 superior barons that ran all of China's 34 provinces on behalf of the Great Khan. Each had their own clerics and judges who resided in the Sheng Palace along with the barons and appointed local governors and other officials for the provinces they were entrusted. Only the Khan stood above them. Kublai's ceremonial guard consisted of 12,000 horsemen split in four units of 3,000 men. One unit was on Palace duty for three days and nights, while the others were dispersed throughout the city, free at night, and then the units rotated. Each member of the guard was a baron and each had as a gift 13 "stupendously expensive" robes of different color: one for each month of the lunar calendar when the Khan would have a feast, one that all 12,000 were invited to attend.

Marco Polo was more than impressed by the parties that were held at the palace, sometimes with as many as 40,000 guests attending. On one occasion, the Khan hosted a party and received a gift of over 100,000 white horses. The palace was certainly capable of housing such a high number as it also employed 20,000 falconers, 10,000 dog trainers and had a 'circus' of tigers, leopards and around 5,000 elephants, all robed in the finest silk of gold and silver. It is mind-blowing just to think of such scale and grandeur, and it all disappeared around 600 years ago with the Empire's demise. Many thought it had gone for good, but only a decade ago, some remnants and ruins were discovered under the Forbidden City in Beijing. The latter was built in 1416, and if you have the chance to visit, then it really is a true wonder; and knowing that Kublai's palace is immediately under your feet, where Marco Polo feasted and saw the Khan accept 100,000 white horses as a New-Year present, makes for a really great experience.

Outside the city walls, there were the suburbs, where even more people lived and plenty of inns would provide accommodation to travelers attracted either by the city's great market or by seeking favor or office with the Khan's court. An immense number of luxury goods would find their way into Khanbaliq as Polo recounts: pearls, precious stones, gold and silk cloth, spices, etc. Such was the number of people surrounding the city, constantly incoming and outgoing that Marco accounts there were approximately 20,000 prostitutes to satisfy demand (though they were forbidden to work within the city's walls).

This was also the place where he first saw how people burned certain special black stones that they dug from the mountains and he recounts that these stones would burn better and longer than wooden logs; although later it was discovered to be abundant in Europe, coal was yet unheard of and Marco Polo's book might well be the first written European source about it.

Khanbaliq was also the seat of the emperor's mint. Marco Polo was amazed to witness for the first time how "paper" currency was produced. They would remove the thin layer of bast that was situated between the bark and the trunk of a mulberry tree; this was then ground, pounded and pressed with glue forming a large sheet of "paper", which was completely black; this sheet was in turn cut into pieces of different size, each size representing a different denomination and each bearing the emperor's stamp; Marco accounted for at least 12 different denominations. In this day and age, currency consisted largely of gold, silver and bronze or copper coins and the value of the currency was ultimately locked into the very material of which they were made. So it was truly amazing that a certain piece of bast pressed with glue, would hold the value of a gold bezant (the largest denomination was equal to ten gold bezants[23]) and people would willingly accept that exchange. It was true that it had the Khan's stamp on it and therefore the Khan's (and his cavalry's) guarantee; but it was also backed by gold. Several times a year, the Khan would issue a proclamation for all the gold, silver and precious stones in the city

---

[23] Originally, bezants were 24-carat golden coins used largely across Europe and the Middle East; the hyperpyron was minted in Byzantium, and gold dinars (or "Saracen bezants") were minted in Jerusalem and Tripoli. In Marco Polo's times, they were already debased to 18, or even 15 carats, while he was traveling across China. To put the currency in perspective, a blacksmith in Constantinople would make 15-20 hyperpyron a year.

to be brought to the Mint, where they were exchanged for currency; merchants would also bring the valuable metals and stones from far flung corners of the empire and exchange them for the paper currency. So the Mint was effectively in control of the majority of the gold and silver in circulation and could exchange it back (or not) for currency. For example, if a citizen wanted to buy silver or gold to have a necklace made for his wife, he could purchase it at face value from the Mint in exchange for currency. In theory, this sounds like the Gold Standard we had in the past century; in practice, I very much doubt the Mint was going to be capable of honoring its commitments if all outstanding currency bills were simultaneously submitted for exchange.

The expenses of the court were eye-watering; 10,000 trainers for the Khan's dogs, 40,000 servants for his wives, lavish parties and hunting expeditions. But it wasn't all wasted on splendor and luxuries. The Yuan dynasty maintained a very sophisticated road network and postal service. On the main roads that lead into every province, there were post stations situated at every 25-30 miles and each of these represented a "large and splendid palace," which had the capacity to lodge foreign dignitaries or province governors along with their suite; common travelers were also welcomed so long as they could pay and strict logs were kept of every visitor's name and dates of stay. Stations were found and maintained even in far flung mountainous roads (though they were less frequent there). And every station maintained 300-400 horses. That way when the Khan sent a courier, they could change horses at every station and thus travel 250-300 miles per day. Marco Polo recounts he'd never seen anything like this. It was a network of 10,000 palaces, strung throughout the entire realm, including in uninhabited areas, and looking after at least 200,000 horses. And as if that wasn't enough, the empire maintained small (40-house) villages at every three miles between the post stations, where unmounted couriers lived. They would put on large belts, covered with bells, and sprint with a message for three miles to the next village. The bells would make a great noise, so that a running courier could be heard from afar in the next village, another courier would prepare upon hearing the noise, take the message that is passed, then sprint for another three miles and so on. In this manner, the Khan could receive a message within 24 hours from a place that was 10 days' journey away. In truth, the system was also used to deliver fresh fruit to him. Furthermore, there were trees planted on the sides of the roads: this provided invaluable shadow and cool in the hot summer months, and made it virtually impossible for a traveler to go astray of the road in the winter months.

And in case you think that he was probably taxing the hell out of everybody, this postal system was used to bring the Khan reports from around the empire. And when the Khan would find out about a crop failure, he would not only exempt the province from the year's taxes but would send them grain from his own silos to ensure they would have enough to eat and to sow. The Khan would maintain huge reserves of grain as he would purchase excess amounts during bumper crops that could be maintained for three or four years: wheat, barley, rice, millet, etc. Same tax-exemption and state-support principles applied to herds, flocks and ship cargo (particularly if the ship was struck by lightning). On top of that, Marco Polo recounts that the Khan took care of the poor and hungry families in Khanbaliq, particularly those with many children, by providing them with barley and other staples, so they did not go hungry; and his court would take on about 30,000 people daily asking for bread and all of them received a portion.

# CHAPTER IX
# LIFE AND TRAVELS IN CHINA

## The Wonders of Tibet

Kublai Khan was ruling a vast empire and had interest in every corner of it, and not just a ruler's interest into the strategic or operational issues, nor even for the sake of being aware of local politics and intrigue. He had deep interest in the people who lived there, their habits, their culture, their religion, crafts, trade and general way of living; he was also interested in the wildlife and landscapes of the lands. Most envoys he would send to far flung provinces, however, did not seem to comprehend that and would provide him with reports that would contain only matters of immediate interest to their mission, such as crop yields, taxation or other administrative issues. Having listened to Marco Polo's descriptions of the lands he had passed through on his way to China, Kublai quickly decided to make him an envoy and then sent him to the southwestern-most part of the Yuan dynasty lands. This was Marco Polo's first trip in China, which he made in the span of four months and without the company of his father or uncle.

His first impressions began just ten miles outside of Khanbaliq, where he crossed Yongding River, a tributary to Hai River, which at the time was named Pulisanghin and served as a major waterway for local merchants' cargo boats. What caught young Polo's attention was a beautiful bridge that was constructed in a way he had not seen: it was made entirely out of gray marble with 24 arcs and 24 piers in the water, it was eight paces (six meters) wide and 300 paces (230m) long, which meant that ten horsemen could cross it side by side with ease. Polo was impressed with the piers' design: every pier of the bridge was shaped like the bow of a ship to split the water more effectively and they faced both down and upstream (as high tides would sometimes result in strong reverse currents). He was also amazed by the fine craftsmen work done on the bridge's handrails that consisted of hundreds of marble figures of lions, each in a different stature. The bridge stands on the Yongding to this day and is known as the Marco Polo Bridge. It was in fact the site where the Second Sino-Japanese War started on July 7th 1937 with a clash between China's National Revolutionary Army and the Imperial Japanese Army, who was searching for a missing soldier and was refused passage to search the town of Wanping.

Riding west, Marco Polo passed through what he described as a beautiful countryside with lots of splendid vineyards, fertile fields and civilized homes and inns along the way. Among the main crafts in these lands was the weaving of fine silk and gold fabrics, particularly a fine thin one called sendal. After a ten-day ride, he reached the province of Taiyuan Fu, renowned for its wonderful wine that was exported throughout all of Cathay.

This province was also an industrial center, where a great deal of the military equipment for the Kahn's army was produced.

Further on Marco Polo passed through Xiuzhou Castle, built by a mystical historical figure known as the Golden King. There he marveled at the splendid great hall, whose walls were covered by marvelous paintings of all the kings who once ruled the province. Then on to what he called the Qara Muren River (but was really the Yellow River), so wide and deep that no bridge was yet made to cross over it in the 13th century. Marco marveled at the market towns strung on its banks, the vast number of boats that crisscrossed it, the excessive number of birds that could be found and the variety of spices, some of which were never even heard of in Europe; and as always, there was an abundance of gold and silk fabrics.

To the south of the Yellow River, Marco Polo passed through the rich kingdom of Chang'an. He describes it as a land of Buddhists, rich with gardens, fields, birds and game, with thriving trade and industry, where all kinds of military equipment were produced along with fine silk cloths. It boasted a castle, situated within fortified walls about as large as the Khan's, with walls illustrated on the inside with beaten gold. Chang'an was ruled by Manggala, the second son of Kublai and Chabi, his first wife; Marco Polo describes him as a just ruler, loved by the people, under whom the kingdom flourished and everything people needed was available at low cost.

After a three-day ride, Marco and his companions reached the mountains and the province of Gangyuan. The mountains were of low elevation and had plenty of small villages with inns where they could lodge. The people would live by farming, forestry and hunting and the forests were teeming with stags and roe deer but also with tigers, lynxes and bears. They spent around 20 days traveling across these mountains until they reached a large fertile plain, where Marco recounts plenty of ginger was produced and exported throughout Cathay provinces. After crossing that plain, they carried on through mountainous terrain but the elevations became somewhat higher until they reached the city of Chengdu Fu. Marco Polo recounts that the city was divided into three parts by inner walls because before the Mongols took it, its king divided it in equal parts among his three sons. Several large rivers ran through this city and joined outside its walls to form the mighty Yangtze River. He marveled at the many great bridges, covered with decorated red roofs and lined with market booths where all sorts of wares were traded and considerable levies were collected. Marco notes the vastness of the Yangtze River and the great number of vessels that swarmed it even at this early stage of its flow in what we call today the Sichuan mountains.

They carried on through the mountains and reached Tibet. As Marco Polo recounts, the country had been completely devastated by the ravages of the Mongols, and most of it was desolate with little in the way of food and water. The outskirts were apparently infested with all kinds of dangerous wild beasts that had to be fended off by using the loud cracking sounds of bamboo canes. He describes the widest bamboo canes he'd seen thus far and while traveling through the mountains, they would throw them into their fire, where the bamboo would crack with such a loud sound that would scare all animals within a 10-mile radius.

After spending 20 days traveling through the Tibetan mountains without any lodging, they finally reached a region with plenty of villages, where he found some of the practices interesting. The Tibetans didn't use the Khan's paper money as currency, but instead used salt. They also valued coral and amber, which they would put around the necks of their wives and idols. He was amazed by their large mastiffs (the size of donkeys) and mentions an abundance of musk deer they hunted. He also saw the methods of cleaning asbestos, which was at the time being used in Suchow extensively. Apparently, the easiest way of dealing with it was to put it on a fire; a practice which thankfully didn't continue for too long. Polo describes the locals as completely depraved and the greatest rascals and thieves in the world. They lived by hunting, breeding cattle, and subsistence farming, but would also not find it sinful to commit a robbery. This strangely contradicts the modern image we have of the Tibetan nation and it is not clear whether it was Polo's narrative or some monk's editorial, outraged with another interesting local habit that particularly intrigued Polo.

In the 13th century (and well before and after too), Tibetan men had nothing but total contempt for women who were still virgins. This completely different viewpoint from Western culture was because they believed that if a woman hadn't had sex with numerous men, it was because they were cursed by God (or gods as Polo described). A man would never marry a virgin, as she was clearly not good enough to find a mate, so there were the almost comical – but ultimately rather sad – scenes of mothers running to any male visitor and offering their daughters for sex, so that in the future she could find a man who

126

would marry her. Once that had taken place, the traveler would then give the young girl a jewel or some other token and as the custom went, the girl could start thinking about marriage once she had collected at least 20 of these. Of course, the more tokens she had, the better her chances of marriage. It is shocking to our Western point-of-view, and to a certain extent Polo's too, but it was entirely normal in Tibet. A word of warning here: if you are a single male, please DO NOT go to Tibet expecting the custom to still be in use. You may be disappointed, and you may also find yourself in serious trouble.

## The Wonders of Pagan

The next province of Jiandu offered yet stranger sexual habits. Tibetan girls may be offered to strangers before they were married, but once wed, it was considered a great crime to sleep with another man's wife. Contrary to that, in Jiandu, if a stranger approached a house in search of a place to stay, the man would vacate the house and leave the stranger to bed his wife. As per the custom, the stranger should put his hat on the door or on some visible place to alert the man of the house that he was still in, and would stay on for three days (or perhaps longer), while the man of the house was someplace else (with someone else's wife in some nearby village?). Other than that, Marco describes it as a rich province with plenty of cloves, ginger, and cinnamon as well as plenty of spices, unseen in Europe at the time; and he seems to have liked the local wine, which was made of rice, wheat, and spices. He also describes a salt lake full of so many pearls that the Khan prohibited the locals from extracting them under penalty of death because the quantities were so vast that the normal pearl's prices would collapse. There were also plenty of turquoise stones in the mountain but like the pearls, they could only be touched when sanctioned by the Khan.

The next province of Qarajang (modern-day Yunnan) also offered strange habits. Sleeping with another man's wife was considered normal as long as there was consent from her; and people seemed to enjoy eating their meat raw, especially the livers, mixed well with garlic sauce. The ruler was another of Kublai's sons, Yisun Temur, and the capital, Yachi, was a bustling market with plenty of merchants and artisans, where cowries (white shells, imported from India) could be used as currency. This is the place where Marco Polo saw pythons for the first time and he was understandably awed by these mighty serpents that could eat a man alive. He describes how local hunters buried wooden poles with large iron hooks on steep riverbanks and when the python rushed down the banks for water, it would rip itself open and die. The locals used its skin and meat (which was delicious, according to Marco) and also produced medicine from the snake's gall, which would be used for things as diverse as skin sores, rabid bites, and labor pains.

Going further west, Marco Polo entered the province of Zardandan, which was already in modern-day Burma. Gold was abundant in these lands and cheaper than elsewhere and men would cover their teeth with gold. As there were no silver mines around, the locals would exchange gold for silver at a 1:5 rate, while elsewhere throughout the empire, the normal exchange rate was 1:8. Therefore plenty of traders would come about for a profitable purchase of gold. Marco was also bemused by the lack of physicians (though those familiar with the physicians in Medieval Europe may consider this a blessing); when someone fell ill, a gang of sorcerers would come and trance until one of them dropped flat on his back and foam flowed from his mouth. They would talk to the spirits with him and determine whether the ill could be cured or not and if they could be cured, what needed to be sacrificed. This usually resulted in an instruction to sacrifice some number of sheep and prepare some number of drinks, so friends and family would gather to fulfill the instructions; there would be sacrifice, there would be cooking, there would be broth and beverage sprinkling around the house, then there would be a party and then the ill would (hopefully) recover. Beats leeches any day if you ask me.

The Khan had only recently joined Zardandan into his empire when in 1272 he won a battle with the king of Myanmar and Bengal over its capital, Yongchang. The 12,000 Mongol horsemen faced a force of 2,000 elephants, each with a wooden castle on top with between 12 and 16 people manning it and an additional 60,000 troops, both cavalry and foot soldiers. But as the elephants approached on the plain and the Mongols saw their horses terrified, they had no choice but to run and hide in a nearby grove, where they tied them to the trees. Then, using the cover of the trees, they unleashed an unstoppable rain of arrows on the elephants until one by one they began falling or turning back and running through and over the Bengali foot soldiers, then into the surrounding forests where most of the castles atop their backs were smashed in the trees. The Mongols charged with their horses amid the chaos that the elephants caused on the plain while running in terror. The battle continued for the good part of the day, but in the end, the Mongols were victorious and even managed to catch 200 of the elephants by using the skills of some of the captured Bengalis to trap them in the forest. And this was when Kublai Khan took a great interest and began using elephants in his army.

From the hilly jungles of Zardandan, Marco Polo descended for a couple of days down towards the province of Myanmar, which bordered India. There he describes thick jungles full of elephants and "unicorns," which is how he named the rhinoceros he had never before seen in his life, and a total lack of houses or villages on the way for fifteen days. He then reached the city of Pagan, which had by this time become part of the Mongolian empire. He describes the king's tomb, which had two identical towers – one layered with gold and one layered with silver, with the layers having the thickness of a thumb, both towers laden with gilded bells that would ring whenever the wind blew. The tomb was left untouched by orders of the Khan out of respect to its beauty and Pagan's dead king.

Pagan was the terminus of Marco Polo's first trip throughout China though he does narrate about the province of Bengal, which was not yet conquered by the Khan but according to Marco, conquest was imminent. What he mentions is that Bengal had plenty of cotton and spices such as galangal, ginger and spikenard as well as the fact that they were the marketplace of choice if you were looking to buy eunuchs or slave girls. He then describes several provinces as he traveled eastwards back into China via a different route, where there was plenty of gold and people used gold and the aforementioned cowries as currency. The trip took him approximately two months through these lands, where he saw tribes that had their bodies covered in tattoos, ones that would wear their wealth as golden bracelets on their arms and legs and a lewd province king who would marry any girl that caught his eye, resulting in a grand total of 300 wives (in the Kingdom of Champa in modern-day Vietnam). Local diets consisted primarily of meat, milk and rice along with the ubiquitous local wine made of rice and spices.

In the end, he made it to the city of Fuling, already in China proper on the upper reaches of the Yangtze River, and where the Khan's paper money was used for trade. This province was teeming with tigers and it was dangerous to sleep out in the open or even in boats if too close to shore for the tigers would climb on the boat and snatch people at night. This was where Marco Polo witnessed how the locals were hunting tigers with a local breed of dogs that were big, ferocious and trained to fight with the tigers. A mounted man would set the dogs on the tiger and they would attack from two sides, front and back, while the tiger would twist and turn in an attempt to harm either of them, but the well trained dogs would manage to evade its claws. Eventually the tiger would back up towards a tree to face the two dogs with its back protected. At this point the man would start shooting his arrows at the animal, which would be trapped and have no means of escaping. Fuling was a trading center with plenty of silk and other wares sold and ferried on the river. Then a 12-day journey along the riverbanks took Marco back to Chengdu Fu, where his party had already been on its way south.

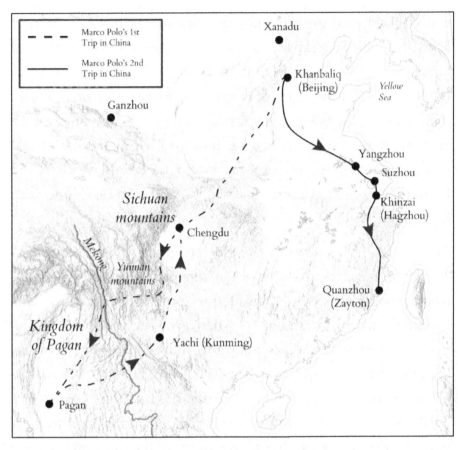

*Marco Polo's First China Trip*

## The Mangi

Back in Khanbaliq, Marco Polo remained in service of the Great Khan and would set out on numerous trips as the Khan's envoy. Apart from the missions he served, he also became a favorite of the Khan as he would always entertain him with observations and stories coming as first-eye accounts from the lands he visited. Kublai also had a great interest in Europe and as Polo was the only European in court with such a high rank, it was probably palpable for the other nobles that the young man had been somewhat more favored by the Khan. Recent findings in the Chinese chronicles of the Yuan dynasty reveal with a level of certainty that Marco Polo ran into trouble in Khanbaliq around 1282 when he unknowingly escorted two ladies in the Imperial Palace during the dark part of the day, when by law men and women had to walk separately. An ambitious young courtier who was a confidant of the Khan ordered his arrest and Polo was led to the Khan for a sentence. Having heard the case, Kublai Khan not only pardoned Marco Polo but entrusted him with a mission to act as his tax collector in the eastern province of Yangzhou. What the Khan really wanted was to get Polo out of sight as he had already drawn too much ire from the nobles, while at the same time taking advantage of Polo's unbiased and skillful reports from far flung provinces. But the decision felt deeply humiliating to the courtier who ordered Marco Polo's arrest, so deep that he turned to alcoholism and died in short order, causing serious discontent among high officials in the court. This was how Marco Polo's second China trip started, and this time he was accompanied by his father and uncle who also became targets of the Chinese courtiers' animosity in Khanbaliq.

So the Polos set out south on another long journey but they already felt uneasy in these foreign lands. They were worrying about what may happen to them should the Khan pass away. In any case, Kublai Khan had appointed Marco Polo to act as his tax collector, so going back to Europe was not yet in the offing. Instead they traveled south and southeast through lands they had not yet seen, under the shade of the trees that were planted by orders of the Khan on the side of the roads. A week away from Khanbaliq they witnessed first-hand the extraction of salt in Changlu in a manner different from the usual technology whereby seawater was gathered in vast basins, brined and evaporated until only the salt remained. The locals would pile a special type of soil that was extremely salty and would drench it in water; the water would then pass through the soil and extract the salt from it; once sufficient concentration was reached, the brine would then be collected into vast containers and boiled to obtain very pure, white and fine-grained salt. As they proceeded further south Marco describes towns and provinces of great riches like silks, spices and jewelry, as well as fertile lands. They passed through the city of Dongpin Fu, a site of a large rebellion against Kublai Khan just ten years prior. He then describes the city of Xinzhou, which was a thriving market city, bustling with river boats. The locals had split the river and it flowed southeast towards Cathay and southwest towards Mangi[24] and in Marco Polo's words these canals bore "such a huge number of vessels that no one would credit it without seeing it." Coming from a person who grew up in Venice, that certainly meant something. But really, nothing in Europe or the Middle East could compare with the Emperor's Canal, a mammoth engineering project done centuries ago and linking the Yellow and Yangtze rivers.

Throughout the journey, Marco Polo mostly describes rich and fertile lands, bustling with trade and crafts, river towns teeming with boats and a Buddhist population who burned their dead and used the Khan's paper currency to trade. And all households

---

[24] Mangi, or Manzi, means "Barbarians of the South" in Chinese and was a derogatory term used to describe the lands of the Song dynasty. Throughout his accounts Marco Polo uses this name to denote the lands that Kublai had recently taken from the Song, but he uses it merely as a name without any hint of disdain.

would keep a record of the names of their men, women, children and slaves on the doors of their house along with the number of horses they kept; newborns were added and the deceased were struck off, which kept the Khan's emissaries somewhat informed about the local population. The closer they got to the Ocean Sea, the larger the boats he described. Before entering the province of Mangi, which was surrounded by lakes and rivers, he witnessed no less than 15,000 vessels all belonging to the Great Khan, that were likely stationed in Hongze lake and could ferry his armies to the islands in the sea, itself a daytrip away from this lake. Each boat could carry a crew of 20 men and transport fifteen horses, their riders and provisions. The province of Mangi was itself taken by the Khan in 1268 and Marco Polo describes it as a place of great wealth, bringing in a "stupendous" amount of revenue to the Khan.

As the story went, Mangi was so difficult to conquer, surrounded as it was by lakes and rivers, that its inhabitants had no combat skills to speak of. Its king's astrologer had said that the province would only ever fall to a man with one hundred eyes. It so happened that the baron sent by Kublai Khan to take this province was named Bayan Chingsang, which meant Bayan Hundred-Eyes[25]. Bayan managed to conquer 12 cities before setting his sights on Xingzai, the capital of the province. The king Facfur, who was no warrior, fled the capital with 1,000 ships to the islands in the Ocean Sea but his queen stayed with a large force, determined to defend the capital. However, when she learned what the name of Kublai's commander was, she promptly

---

[25] And he was not a blind Chinese monk, as portrayed by the Netflix Marco Polo TV show, but a general from the Mongol Baarin tribe.

remembered the astrologer's prophecy and decided to surrender. She was treated with respect and as a royalty by Kublai, but her king was left isolated on the islands where he later perished.

One city in this province, Xiang Yang Fu, however held for another three years. As it was surrounded by lakes from all sides except the north, the Mongols could not lay an effective siege upon it. The locals would use the canals to bring in goods within the city's walls and the Mongol army could not secure the waterways. When the Polos heard of the siege upon their arrival in Khanbaliq, they vowed that they had a way to make the city fall. As already mentioned, they introduced trebuchets to the Great Khan, capable of hurling 300-pound stones to the city's walls. As the Khan's engineers built these weapons outside the walls and began launching stones at a great distance that destroyed house after house, the defenders of the city eventually decided to surrender.

## The Great River Cities

After a journey of nearly 40 days, the Polos finally reached the city of Yangzhou, a day's trip away from the coast and situated on the banks of the Emperor's Canal. Yangzhou was the hub of the salt trade and the seat of one of the twelve highest ranking barons of the Great Khan; a huge center with taxing authority over 27 other great cities, all of them major markets within their own rights and bustling with great trade. This was the destination of Marco Polo who would spend the next three years as a special representative of the Khan with a high rank within the Tax and Salt Authority. Salt here was also leached from the special mineral rich soils as already described but the quantities were so vast that the annual tax from only one of the 27 districts under Yangzhou equaled around 27 tons of gold. So, a Constantinople blacksmith would earn about 20 hyperpyron a year, each weighing about 4.5 grams, or 90 grams in total and Khanbaliq's court would collect salt taxes (only salt taxes, mind you) from this region worth on average 730 tons of gold or the equivalent of what more than eight million blacksmiths would earn. Come to think of it, 10,000 dog trainers then doesn't sound like much of an extravaganza, does it?

While in Yangzhou, Marco traveled across the provinces and made some descriptions of the things he saw. 15 miles to the southeast he marveled at the city of Zhengzhou at the mouth of the giant Yangtze River. Having seen the river to the west during his earlier trip, he was now able to witness its full might. As he recounts, this river was at times ten miles wide and a 120-day trip long. In the city of Zhengzhou, which he describes as a city of no significant size, he witnessed no less than 15,000 vessels coming in and out to trade at any given day. It ran through 16 provinces, it had no less than 200 towns strewn on its banks and, according to Marco Polo, the number of people that lived alongside it, the number of vessels that floated on its waters and the quantity and value of all of their cargo, exceeded everything all the rivers and seas of Christendom had.

Guazhou, also on the Yangtze River, had huge storage facilities for grain and rice. It was the principal supplier of grain to Khanbaliq via the Emperor's Canal (today China's Grand Canal). This massive engineering project was started back in the 6th century by the Sui dynasty as a means to unite the lands of northern and southern China by connecting the great river basins of the Yellow and Yangtze rivers. Parts of it have been constructed a millennium beforehand but it was the Sui dynasty that first connected its various sections into an integrated project. The canal was later expanded and improved upon by the Tang and Song dynasties, including by an innovative pound lock system that the Songs introduced in the 10th century and that made traveling upstream easier and safer. The canal had in later centuries fallen prey to the constant skirmishes between the Jin and the Song dynasties. In 1128, Song governor Du Chong, broke down the dikes and dams that held the Yellow River in an attempt to repel the advancing Jin armies from the northeast. This had the net effect of changing the river course south and dilapidating the canal. It was only in the 1270s and 80s when the Mongols, having conquered these lands and after Kublai moved their capital to Khanbaliq when its restoration and expansion began anew. At the time Marco Polo witnessed the greatness of this project, it was nearly 1,800km long, linking lakes, rivers and artificially enlarged ponds, and was used to transport bulk cargo like wheat and coal from the south to the north and vice versa (and this transportation continues nowadays). It was nothing like he'd ever seen in Europe or elsewhere. And it is not clear if he had found out that the canal was in existence before anyone in Europe even thought about Venice[26].

The city of Zhenjiang Fu, also on the banks of the Yangtze River, caught Marco's attention with its two churches of Nestorian

---

[26] This is an exaggeration because it is widely accepted that Venice was found in the 5th century by refugees fleeing the open Italian grounds from Atilla. Still, most of the Chinese canals were dug way earlier, and in the 5-6th century Venice was merely a fishermen's village.

Christians built in 1278 by Governor Mar Sergius, who had been appointed by the Khan for three years. Never before, according to Marco Polo, had there been any churches in these parts of the world or even a single believer in Christ. In fact, the first Christians that came to the city were conquerors, dispatched by no other but the aforementioned Banyan Hundred-Eyes, namely a large contingent of Alans whom he used in the conquest of the province of Mangi. The Alans captured the city with ease but found the local wine so delightful that they got themselves drunk into stupor and then the locals slayed them all pretty much in their sleep. This drew Banyan's ire and he put a vast majority of the locals to the sword, so the population was still undergoing a recovery when Marco Polo arrived. Nevertheless, as in all other parts of the provinces he describes a vibrant city, bustling with trade and crafts, amidst rich and fertile lands, populated mostly by Buddhists, relatively safe and using the Khan's paper money.

One of the greatest cities of the area, situated near the estuary of the Yangtze, was Suzhou. It was a huge city that Marco describes to be sixty miles around, a bustling market center where tons of gold silk fabrics would change hands daily. As he saw it, if the inhabitants were men-at-arms, there would be no army in the world that could stop them, so vast were their numbers, but he describes the locals as "men without courage;" still, he admits he found among them many skilled merchants and craftsmen as well as plenty of philosophers and natural physicians. He counted 6,000 stone bridges in the city, large enough to have two galleys pass below them. The name of the city translates as "Earth" but Marco was even more amazed when he visited the city whose name, Xingzai (modern-day Hangzhou), translated as "Heaven." As he would describe it, this city was "the finest and noblest in the world;" it was a hundred miles in circumference and had 12,000 stone bridges, under which a galley could pass (so double the number of Suzhou). The city was connected to the sea via a canal but situated amidst a lake and as it was linked to the land only by bridges it was relatively secure from (non-Mongol) invasion. The city was a magnificent center of commerce and industry with twelve guilds for separate crafts, each possessing at least 12,000 workshops each employing at least ten men and in some cases twenty or even forty – apprentices, journeymen and masters. The people were wealthy and their favorite pastime was spending time with their spouses and families as well as bathing in the numerous fountains and lakes strewn in the area. And Polo accounts for at least 3,000 hot baths where people would go and bathe at least several times a month (given the hygiene habits in Europe at the time, this must have been a stretch to believe). They would hold weddings or banquets in especially fit-for-purpose palaces with pottery, linen, and flatware that surrounded a nearby beautiful lake, 30 miles in circumference (the West Lake). Around the lake he witnessed "… an endless procession of pleasure seekers, for people in the city think of nothing else but to spend part of the day with their womenfolk enjoying themselves; for their minds and thoughts are intent upon nothing but the delights of society." He also made a note of the stone towers, especially made for people to escape fires, which were a frequent occurrence back in those days, when the majority of the houses were made of wood. There was even a tower atop a hill in the center of the city, where a guard would keep constant watch and beat an enormous drum if he spotted a fire breaking out.

Marco Polo estimates this city and its immediate district alone would provide tax revenue from salt, sugar, spices, silk, wine, coal and all of the crafts' guilds of about 92 tons of gold[27], roughly a quarter of which coming from the salt tax. As rebellions against the Khan would still occur every now and then, there were plenty of the Khan's troops stationed within every major city and town from ten to up to thirty thousand in cities like Xingzai and Fuzhou. The latter was the capital of the neighboring province, six days to the southeast of Xingzai and six days to the west of the port of Zayton (the Chinese name of this port was Quanzhou but Marco Polo chose to use the Persian name Zayton throughout his book). The province of Fuzhou impressed Marco with the size of its bamboo and the abundance of tigers who would attack travelers in broad daylight; and with the local fierce soldiers who would drink the blood and eat the meat of men they killed in battle. There, he also saw hens that had no feathers but fur ("like cats") and laid eggs ("very good to eat") just like normal hens. Plenty of sugar, ginger, saffron, camphor, galangal and silk were produced in this province. And in the city of Fuzhou, plenty of river-going vessels were built. This was also a large trading center, linked to the sea by the river canals, and Marco saw plenty of ships coming in from India, past the port of Zayton and up the river to the market of Fuzhou, carrying various wares.

---

[27] He uses the measure of tomans of gold (290 in this case), which is a Persian unit, since most of the tax administrators in the Khan's tax authority were Persians.

Zayton, to the southeast was the principal port where the bulk of the trade with India would take place and tons of merchandise, pepper, aloes, sandalwood, pearls and precious stones would enter China (some of it carried directly via the canal to Fuzhou, six days inland). It was likewise also the main point of exports from the Mangi province and a big part of China. In Marco Polo's words, this was the busiest port he'd ever seen and as he put it, for every ship loaded with pepper that left from the Indies for a Christian port, one hundred such ships arrived at Zayton, so busy was the traffic he witnessed. And all the ships coming from India were liable to pay a 10% tax on their cargo to the Khan, so the revenue streams must have been mind boggling. Still, despite the taxes and the freight costs that together approached or exceeded 50% of the cargo's value, the number of incoming ships was bigger than what the young Venetian had ever seen. Apart from silk, gold, spices and various crafted goods, this province was the production center of porcelain bowls that, as Marco recounts, were exceptionally beautiful and were not produced anywhere else in the empire.

# CHAPTER X
# THE LONG ROAD TO HOME

## Princess Kokochin and the Malay Islands

By the year 1291, the Polos had spent 17 years in the Khan's service. By this time, the Khan was already 76 years old, which was quite an old age. The Polos had no doubt amassed wealth during their tenure in China but they were also awed by the great power the Khan swayed over every subject in this land. They were well aware that the court in Khanbaliq was not as well disposed towards them as the Khan was and they could not help but worry what would become of them when he inevitably passed away. For the next Great Khan would hold unlimited power not only over their wealth but over their lives. They had already asked Kublai several times to allow them to return to Europe but he refused under different pretexts.

Apparently he decided that their time had come when a delegation from the Ilkhanate arrived at Khanbaliq[28]. Arghun

---

[28] The ambassadors Marco Polo named in his accounts were Oulatai, Apusca and Coja. The names of this delegation were also found in 15th century Chinese chronicles and, even though there was no mention of the Polos in these chronicles, this can be considered a proof of the veracity of Polo's accounts.

Khan of the Ilkhanate, son of Abaqa, the nephew of Kublai, had sent three ambassadors on a special mission to the Great Khan. His beloved wife Bolgana had died in 1286 and he insisted that only one of her kinswomen should inherit her. She belonged to the Mongol Bayaut tribe and Kublai chose for his nephew the 17-year-old Princess Kokochin[29], a relative of Bolgana. In that same year however, the Chagatai Khanate unexpectedly attacked the Ilkhanate. Abaqa Khan had died in 1282 and was at first succeeded by Tekuder, his brother, who was the first Ilkhan to convert to Islam. However he did not push the Islamic agenda in the Ilkhanate as there was serious resistance against it; after all the Mamluks were the enemy. Arghun used this to replace Tekuder and in 1286 he succeeded (with the support of the aforementioned Qara'unas and the blessing of Kublai Khan). The emir of the province of Khorasan however, Narwuz, who was also a Muslim and with very ambitious plans for the province, rebelled against Arghun in 1289. Prior to this rebellion Narwuz was an ally of Arghun against Tekuder and even the atabeg of Arghun's 13-year-old son, Ghazan[30]. Narwuz lost twice to Arghun's armies and had to flee to the Chagatai Khanate straight into the hands of Kaidu[31]. In 1291, the year when Kublai Khan would meet Arghun's delegation, Narwuz invaded Khorasan with the help of Kaidu's armies, led by Kaidu's two sons Sarban and Ebugen. Kublai therefore was convinced by the delegates

---

[29] There are a number of different spellings and translations of her name but it is mostly assumed to mean the "Blue Princess" or "Dove".

[30] This is a Turkic title, which means a subordinate of the monarch, charged with raising the crown prince.

[31] At the time, the throne of the Chagatai Khanate was occupied by Duwa, one of Baraq's sons, but he was appointed by Kaidu who remained the de facto ruler of the Chagatai Khanate until his death in 1301.

that it would be safer for the princes to travel by sea, something the Mongols were not very adept at. They further convinced the Khan that they could make great use of the Polos who were expert seafarers. The Khan eventually submitted and decided to entrust the Polos with the mission of leading the delegation back to Tabriz in the Ilkhanate by sea. He also sent, by the Polos, friendly messages to the European potentates and the king of England.

The modern dramatization of Marco Polo implies a love story between himself and Princess Kokochin but that is highly unlikely to have occurred and there is no shred of evidence for that either. For one thing, the Polos were escorting a princess that was to marry a khan of unlimited power, for another they were traveling by ship and anyone who has spent but a few days on one could tell you that there is no such thing as keeping a secret on a ship. Last, but not least, in 1291 Kokochin was 17 and Marco Polo was 37, so the characters we see on Netflix do not correspond much with reality. In the series Marco meets Kokochin upon his arrival in Khanbaliq; in reality, she wasn't even born at the time. In any case, whether a story occurred or not is not something we can know (or even speculate on), so let's focus on the journey instead.

Unlike the shaky dhows they decided to avoid in Tabriz, the Indian ships they saw in Dayton made quite an impression on the Polos. Their hulls had two layers of planks, all nailed with iron nails and caulked in and out with a special oil, which could only be found in India (unlike pitch, which they did not have). The ships had decks and plenty of spacious cabins on top of it as well as four masts, with additional two that could be raised and lowered as needed; and they also had oars with four-men stations. The larger ones required a crew of up to 200 sailors and could carry five or six thousand baskets of pepper (approx. 600 tons). These ships were accompanied by smaller ones (40-80 crew) that towed them in shallow waters as well as service boats that would lay their anchors, fish and generally service the flotilla.

The Polos set sail with a fleet of 14 ships from Zayton and headed southwest through the Gulf of Tonkin (or the Gulf of Cheynam as Marco dubbed it). At that time, the kingdom of Champa, in modern-day southern Vietnam was paying annual tribute to Kublai Khan, consisting of elephants and aloeswood. In 1278, the Khan's commander Sogatu had difficulties taking the kingdom over as the cavalry was not very efficient in the difficult hilly jungle terrain. The locals were hiding in fortified towns that proved impregnable but the Mongols (and Chinese) could ravage the countryside. Eventually the king sent envoys that offered tribute to the Khan and he agreed to leave Champa alone. The kingdom itself was rich and had plenty of elephants, ebony forests and aloeswood; and the already mentioned lewd king would marry every girl he liked, so when Marco visited the kingdom[32] he found that the king had 326 children, of which 150 were capable men-at-arms. Puts Kublai's offspring in perspective.

---

[32] In fact, Marco Polo had visited the Kingdom in 1285 during his trip to the Kingdom of Pagan. On this trip the flotilla stopped only briefly in the Kingdom of Champa to re-stock.

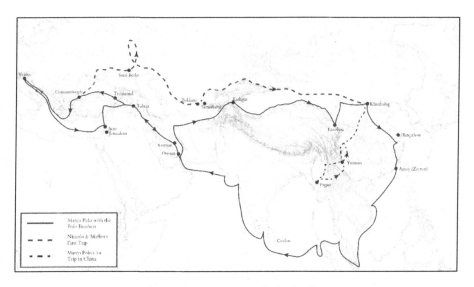

*The Epic Journeys of the Polos*

They then proceeded to the Malay islands and the Strait of Malacca, so far south that for the first time in his life Marco could not see the North Star at night. At the time the islands of Indonesia were not under singular rule as we are accustomed to seeing them today. Rather, they were a patchwork of kingdoms and independent islands, dominated by the kingdoms, seated on the islands of Java and Sumatra. The Indonesian islands were the main source of spice for the entire world and Polo describes the vast riches of Java in terms of nutmegs, pepper, cloves, galangal, cubebs, spikenard and every spice one could ever conceive of. Merchants from China and India would come to this island and make great riches through trade. The treasure found on this island was beyond imagination but it was never conquered by the Mongols because their sea-faring skills were limited and so were those of the peoples they conquered: the Persians built ships that had the Polos (who grew up on water) prefer a two year ride through Pamir and the Taklamakan; and the Chinese, while skilled engineers and inventors of the compass could never get past coastal navigation. It was in fact Kublai's unsuccessful attempts to conquer Japan that marked the peak and the eventual limits of the Mongol expansion.

Marco Polo describes the island of Sumatra and its eight kingdoms, where people were mostly savages, living in the mountain jungles and eating any kind of flesh, including human; certain tribes even had tails about a palm long but with no hair. He notes however that the people living in the ports had accepted Islam, so as to be able to trade with the Muslims. Most of the inhabitants considered themselves subjects to the Khan but paid no tribute to him despite gifts they would send every now and then. This is where he describes a "unicorn," like a really ugly beast with buffalo hair and elephant legs, a thick black horn on the forehead, spikes on the tongue and always prone to wallow in the mud. "A very ugly beast," he concludes, "nothing like the animal we describe in our lands that lets itself be caught only by a virgin." This was of course a Javan rhinoceros. It must have been amazing to walk in these dense forests and see the enormous variety of birds and monkeys they had to show; and it must have been quite dangerous too as there would have also been plenty of snakes and insects. One thing that drew Marco's attention were the apes that he saw. He goes on to explain that the people who claimed to bring "pygmies" in Europe from India (apparently he talks about stuffed mortified bodies) were cheaters. He found that these "pygmies" were produced on this island and were really apes that had a humanoid face, especially prepared by plucking their hair off (except the beard and the chest), dried, stuffed and dabbed in saffron and other spices. They were not small men, as their sellers claimed.

Their fleet stayed on Sumatra for five months to wait out the dangerous Monsoon winds. They disembarked from their ships and built wooden fortified homes to protect themselves from maneaters and wild animals. They ate fish ("best in the world"), rice and coconuts, and discovered how the locals made flour from the fruit of unknown trees, which was heavy and would sink when thrown in water (likely a breadfruit). They also indulged in the local adult beverage that Marco liked very much (just like any other "wine" he describes in his book); it was extracted from the branches of a local small date palm and in all likelihood Marco described what we know today as toddy or palm wine, which is popular in Africa, South and Southeast Asia (though I do recommend rum over it any time anywhere).

In Dagroian, another one of Sumatra's kingdoms, Marco Polo marveled at how they treated the ill. Relatives would call the local magicians to determine if the person would live or die and they would perform a ritual, the gist of which was putting some cloth over the ill's mouth, so they would suffocate and die. Then they cooked and ate him or her and all the relatives took part in the feast until the man or woman was eaten whole, including their bone marrow because according to their belief if any flesh was left, it would generate worms and the worms would die, which would expose their soul for torment. Picture this: an in-law passes by and asks you how's your health and you are left wondering if they were just being polite or planning a barbecue for the weekend.

Marco Polo proceeds to describe the crossing of the Strait of Malacca along with the kingdoms of Lochac (southern Thailand, where plenty of cowries came from), Malayu (on the island of Bintan, sitting astride the Strait), Nicobar (where men and women ran naked) and Andaman (where they sharpened their teeth). He also brought in some seeds of brazilwood (used to extract a certain crimson dye) to try and grow in Europe but as it turned out, the climate was prohibitive. Then finally they reached the island of Ceylon, lying 10,000 miles to the west, an island where copious amounts of gems were mined: rubies, sapphires, topazes and amethysts but the people wore no clothes (except for rags that covered their private parts).

## Ceylon and the Malabar Coast

It is not clear how long they stayed in Ceylon, but in all likelihood, Marco Polo met with the local king, Sendernam. He was stunned by the marvelous ruby he saw on him and described it to be a palm long and as thick as a man's arm, red as fire and flawless; the most valuable precious stone he had ever seen. The king refused to give it to the Khan's emissaries (sent in 1284) who promised to pay him "the value of a city" in return. I figure it was only distance and the sea that prevented the Khan from making King Sendernam an offer he could not refuse. The emissaries however did not leave empty handed for the king provided them with precious relics, cherished by both Buddhists and Muslims. In the middle of Ceylon, Marco describes a very high mountain, so rocky and steep that it could not be climbed if not for the iron chains lodged in the mountain slopes. And atop of that mountain was the monument of Sakyamuni Burgan who the locals and the Buddhists believed to be the first holy man in whose name idols were made, while the Muslims believed this to be no other than Adam, the first man, and that Adam's grave was also there. As a Christian, Marco dismissed this claim but he did narrate the local story of Sakyamuni Burgan (which means St. Sakyamuni). He was the only son of a powerful king, who spent most of his life in search of God, not tempted by the immense power his father wanted him to inherit and wield, not tempted by worldly affairs and pleasures the palace had to offer, not tempted even by the 30,000 beautiful women his father had him surrounded with to serve every need of his. He chose to live an ascetic life and according to legend died 84 times, each time reincarnating into a different kind of animal until finally he became a god. His monument on the top of the mountain was claimed to have his real hair teeth and eating bowl and King Sendernam presented the Khan's envoys with the bowl, some hair and two molars, which were considered holy and the Khan accepted the gifts with great joy and gratitude. It was later chronicled by the Khan's monks, and confirmed by the Khan himself, that the bowl, made of exquisite green porphyry, when filled with food for one man would provide enough to feed five.

On the southeast coast of India, in a province Marco Polo called Maabar (no L) and is perhaps today's Tamil Nadu, he met another king named Sundara Pandya Devata. He goes to great lengths to describe the rich attire of this king: a collar around his neck, crammed with rubies, sapphires, emeralds and other precious stones, a silk cord hanging from his neck covered with 104 pearls and gems (for the 104 prayers he had to say every morning and evening), gold braces also crammed with jewelry, three on each arm and three on each leg and other pearls and gems on his fingers and toes. The treasure Marco witnessed that this king wore must be worth more than the value of a "substantial" city. That said, his remaining attire was much like everyone else's in the region, i.e. a piece of cloth just covering the family jewels.

The court was immensely rich and in fact, heirs to the throne did not touch the wealth amassed by their predecessor as they felt obliged to procure their own. It wasn't all that challenging: they were mining the gems there and extracted the biggest and best pearls in the world just 60 miles off the coast in April and May, and 300 miles off the coast in September and October. Marco Polo witnessed how the ships would float as Brahmins would charm the fish away and divers would go to depths of up to ten meters in order to extract the pearls from oysters. It would seem the court was not big on math as they would tax 10% of the extracted pearls but would then issue a decree a few times a year when all the pearls on the territory of the kingdom were to be brought to the castle and they purchased them at double prices. They purchased all gems at double prices as well. Then when the king passed away, the new king would not touch the wealth but amass pearls and gems anew. I guess they were not big on logic either. They did like horses, though; the country had none and so they purchased large taboons of 2,000 horses from Arab and Persian merchants. But they had no expertise in caring for the horses, and especially no farriers, so within the span of a year all horses would be dead due to ill-caring and then they would purchase a new taboon; the merchants did not complain and did not bring farriers about. Another habit that stunned Marco was that when dead men were burned, their wives would jump into the fire more often than not, and this was considered a very honorable deed. The king himself had an entourage of barons in his service as well as around 500 wives and concubines, which would all jump in the fire the day he died and his body was burned.

Up to the north in today's Andra Pradesh, Marco Polo claims to have been the only place in the world where diamonds were produced. It was so rich with diamonds that the rain would wash them off the mountain cliffs and people would go and pick them up in the ravines much like mushrooms. This was not without risks for the jungles were teeming with cobras and some ravines were so steep and secluded that men could not climb their walls. White eagles that were also abundant in these lands would help with both problems: they hunted and ate the cobras and the locals found a way to use them to extract diamonds from the dangerous ravines. They basically threw raw meat from the top into the ravines and as it fell, the diamonds that were lying on the ground got lodged into the soft flesh. The eagles would then grab the meat and when they landed somewhere to eat it, the men would chase the bird away and pick the diamonds. They would also sift through their poop as the birds often swallowed the diamonds.

Marco Polo was amazed by many other things in India. For example, they worshiped the oxen and would not eat beef (despite a small sect that would only eat beef if it died of natural causes). When warring, they would weave oxen wool into their horses' manes or their own hair; some would dip their noses in beef dung for good luck. They considered black, not white, to be the divine color and so greased their children with sesame oil, which was produced in great quantities, to darken their skin. And they were very adept at reading omens. For instance, if someone went on a trip but saw somebody else sneezing, then he would sit down and continue no longer unless the person sneezed again. He was particularly amazed by the Brahmins who ate no meat, drank no alcohol, killed no animals, and had no sex with other women than their wives; and especially amazed by their more extreme sect – the Yogis. They chewed a special herb with meals that helped digestion and drank a mixture of sulfur and mercury twice a month, which they claimed prolonged their lives in their god's service. They practiced no bloodletting, which was all the rage in Europe's healthcare at the time. And yet, according to Polo, some of them would live up to 200 years. He did realize that this had to do with their healthy diet, since they ate only plant food and that only when dried (for green fruit and leaves still had souls they figured) and drank nothing but water. They were so obsessed with harming no living souls that they harmed no fleas or flies, or even animals that would attack and kill them. And the reason they gave for burning their dead was that their corpses would breed worms that would die unnecessarily because they would have nothing to eat once they had consumed the body. Just like those people in Sumatra, though the latter did not mind including a soul-bearing uncle or sister on their menu as long as they were sick. The Yogis also wore no clothes at all and claimed that there was nothing shameful in that because they did not use it for sin. In fact, when priests were promoted or ordained they would be stark naked and would have to endure caresses and kisses by a plethora of girls without battering-up. They also believed the oxen to be holy and would on occasion anoint various parts of their body with ox dung. My guess is that Marco Polo was just curious about why they did things in certain ways, which he found bewildering. There is no mention in his writings about trying to convert anyone's faith, which would have been the usual Christian norm back in those days. And there's little wonder. I consider myself an open-minded person but I find it doubtful even in this day and age that I could have a serious theological debate with a priest who sits across from me, not only 100% al fresco but also greased up with cow shit (or bull).

Across the Strait from Ceylon was the port of Kayal (or Kayalpattinam, as is its full name today). Back then it was a very convenient port and a trading post, situated just after rounding the Indian subcontinent, at the gate of the Bay of Bengal and across the narrow strait from Ceylon. It is worth noting that Marco Polo was impressed by the local ruler that maintained high standards of justice and protected the rights of foreign merchants, which was not something common. In the merchant Republic of Venice, these rights were sacrosanct and that was what made it stand out in Europe but in Asia or even elsewhere in Europe that wasn't the case. Just round Cape Comorin at the tip of the subcontinent, on the southern parts of the west coast of India, a ship would try to avoid stopping for re-supply or due to bad weather at all costs. Because the locals would customarily seize all of her cargo with a serene, delightful smile and the self-evident explanation that the merchants must have been heading

155

someplace else but as it happened, God sent this cargo to lucky them, so life was good and they need hold no grudges. Another interesting fact for Kayal's king was that he was the brother of the aforementioned Sundara Pandya Devata; and he had another three brothers, all kings of neighboring provinces. They all had north of 300 wives and all engaged in the involuntary slaughter of a couple of thousand horses per annum. And they often quarreled over all sorts of things, sometimes declaring war on each other, but war never broke out because their mother would put the would-be belligerents in a room and tell them off. If the quarrel was too big and that wouldn't work, she would pull out a knife and threaten suicide by first hacking her own breasts off for having fed such ungrateful little brats and then stabbing herself to death. So that was pretty much how peace talks were successfully conducted in that part of the world.

Marco Polo made a few ports on the west coast of India where he eventually started seeing the North Star again, at first near the horizon and later higher and higher up in the night sky. Along the coast there were various kingdoms and provinces mostly rich in pepper, ginger, cinnamon, cloves, spikenard, brazilwood, incense and indigo (which he watched being produced). The further north one went, the more civilized and the less hot it became. To the more northern parts of the Subcontinent there was production of the finest buckram and the best tanned leather goods in the world. He makes note of their excellent physicians describing them as "adept at keeping a man's body in good health." He also saw plenty of different bewildering animals: monkeys that looked like men, parrots of all kinds of sizes and colors, bigger and better peacocks, hens and pheasants, deer,

156

oxen, rhinos (he called unicorns), elephants, tigers (he called lions), leopards and lynxes. This was where he first saw a black panther, which he also called a lion without realizing it was actually a leopard.

The Malabar coast was famous for its pirates even back then. The predictability of the monsoon winds and ocean currents, the steady flow of merchandise from Arabia and Persia, and the inferiority of the Arabian dhows compared to the ships made in India meant that every year hundreds of pirate ships would set sail from the ports of Malabar, Gujarat and Thane. They sailed in great numbers and confidence even taking their wives and children aboard. The geography of the Arabian Sea allowed for ships to use a wide array of different routes, so the pirates would form a line with their ships, placing them five miles apart, so they could signal each other when they saw potential prey. Some merchants were very well armed and would put up a fight but many would fall into the hands of the pirates. And when they did, the pirates would conduct an extensive search for gold, silver, pearls and precious stones. They would actually have the crew drink an especially prepared mixture of tamarind and sea water, which would have them barf their guts all over the place and the pirates would then check their vomit (and/or excrements) for hidden jewels or pearls. Some seamen were known to have swallowed valuables in order to hide them from pirates when boarded. In the kingdom of Thane (around modern-day Mumbai), the pirates were actually under the king's protection at the time when Marco Polo was there. The number of horses brought into India from Arabia and Persia was so vast that hardly any ship did not carry horses (for the five brothers in the south were far from the only ones buying them in vast quantities). The king of Thane had an agreement with the pirates that they could keep everything from the ships, so long as they brought him all the horses they captured; and they thrived under his protection.

## Coming Home

In 1294, after two years spent in the Indian ocean and 600 lives lost (including two of the three delegates from Tabriz), the flotilla ferrying Princess Kokochin and the Polo family finally reached the port of Hormuz. It is not very clear why so many perished but various speculations suggest scurvy, cholera, pirates and hostile natives (or perhaps a bit of each) as explanations. Without wasting much time, they went back to Tabriz in the same way they came to Hormuz 22 years ago. By the time they arrived, they would have already found out that Kokochin's would-be husband, Arghun, had died in 1291, the same year she left for the Ilkhanate to marry him. On their way, they did make port in India and in Hormuz, and people would have exchanged news like the Ilkhan's death in marketplaces and port taverns. The cause of his death? He befriended a yogi who was very old and very healthy, and shared his secret with him: sulfur and mercury. Arghun's court physician told him that this was not only nonsense, but downright dangerous. It took eight months for the yogi to prove Arghun's physician was right and Arghun passed away, aged 33 in March 1291[33] (after becoming paralyzed in January and

---

[33] This is approximate, but ultimately irrelevant; he was young. Arghun's birth date should be around 1258 according to most sources. The one thing that sheds doubt is Marco Polo's writing about Arghun's battle with Baraq, which must have taken place in 1270, when Arghun would have been aged 12.

Tekuder's widow was executed, accused of witchcraft because of this). I am not certain what happened to the yogi, but I very much doubt he kept his position in the Ilkhan's court.

After Arghun's death, Narwuz broke the alliance with Kaidu as he figured there was no need to use foreign troops but could instead back Uruk Temur, a grandson of Ögedei, for the throne while sponsoring his conversion to Islam. In Khorasan, they faced Ghazan, the son of Arghun and a former apprentice of Narwuz. Uruk Temur married Narwuz's daughter and converted to Islam, but then chose to switch sides the following year and allied with Kaidu (who at the time however was busy with a campaign in northwest India, so did not help in the fight). Meanwhile Tabriz saw another succession struggle with Gayakhtu, a brother of Abaqa and a Muslim, seizing power for two years. Ghazan didn't seem to mind and in fact his uncle Gayakhtu helped him in the fight against Narwuz. It was at this point when Marco Polo and Kokochin arrived in Tabriz. A famine was raging throughout the Ilkhanate at the time and Ghazan happened to be in Tabriz, trying to replenish his forces. It was decided that he would marry Kokochin in his father's stead and after the wedding he hurried back to face Narwuz's forces in Khorasan. Eventually the latter submitted to Ghazan and became his lieutenant.

Later that year Gayakhtu was killed in a palace coup that placed another uncle of Ghazan, named Baidu, a Christian, as Ilkhan. Ghazan and Narwuz led an army that deposed and killed Baidu and Ghazan eventually became one of the most prominent of the Ilkhans and oversaw (no doubt under Narwuz's guidance) the entire Ilkhanate's conversion to Islam. He was also renowned for introducing administrative, agricultural and monetary reforms that stabilized the Ilkhanate's economy and ended the famines, banditry and general instability that plagued the realm. Despite turning to Islam he did not abandon his predecessors' attempts to form a Franco-Mongol alliance against the Mamluks (I imagine in Tabriz they called it Mongol-Frankish alliance) but as we know that did not work. Kokochin became his principal wife when he became Ilkhan but she sadly passed away in 1296, perhaps due to illness; it seems people in the royal court of the Ilkhanate tended to live shortly.

In the meantime, the Polos hurried back to Venice. On February 18, 1294, Kublai Khan passed away, bereft with the loss of his first wife Chabi and his chosen heir Zhenjin, overwhelmed with diabetes, gout, alcoholism, and excessive eating. In March 1294, his grandson, Temur, son of Zhenjin, took over power and subsequently proved to be an able ruler who continued the best practices of his grandfather including tolerance to foreign faiths and cultures but the Polos had no intentions to wait out and see what would happen. News would have made it quick to the Ilkhanate and I guess that they, having made it so close to home and bearing riches that they could part with at the snap of a khan's fingers, did not waste much time hanging around Tabriz; especially since they found themselves amidst a civil war with a famine to boot. In 1291, the year they left Zayton on their way to Hormuz, Acre, the last Christian stronghold on the Levant, fell to the Mamluks and so the best route for the Polos to take was to travel from Tabriz to the Black Sea port of Trebizond on the northern shore of Anatolia. At the time, the kingdom of Trebizond was independent of Mongol rule and their tax authorities robbed (as only tax authorities can) the Polos of much of their wealth. They still retained much of the gems (stitched into their clothes according to some accounts) to be able to finally make a gracious comeback to Venice in 1295. And into another war.

While the previous war between Venice and Genoa had ended with the Treaty of Cremona in 1270 (backed by the need for peace between them for the Eighth and Ninth Crusades), tensions between the two merchant republics had remained high throughout the two decades when the Polos were in China. In 1282 a revolt against Genoan rule in Corsica, led by judge Sinucello, drew the Republic of Pisa (the last of the seven merchant republics that was not yet overcome by Venice or Genoa) into conflict with Genoa. The latter dealt a decisive blow on the Pisan navy in 1284, after which it never really recovered but the important thing was that now, the dominant naval forces remaining in the Mediterranean were Venice and Genoa. Amalfi, Gaeta, Ancona, Ragusa and Pisa had all declined in importance over the centuries mostly due to Venice's natural geographical advantages and later Genoa's geopolitical success. After the defeat of Pisa (Genoa had no interest in taking over the actual republic) it was only a matter of time before war between the remaining two Mediterranean powers broke out. And the fall of Acre in 1291 sped things up (Acre was the original reason for the first war between Venice and Genoa).

The fall of Acre was a devastating blow for Christianity in principle, as it was the last fortress standing against the Mamluks in the Holy Land. For Venice, it had the added effect of cutting it off from supplies of valuable Asian goods like spices.

At the same time, Genoa had kept its trading posts on the Crimean Peninsula in the Black Sea along with significant influence in Constantinople and ports on Lesbos and Thios in the Aegean Sea; so for the first time throughout their history, Genoa appeared to have the upper hand in the Med. Genoan ships began harassing Venetian ships in the eastern Mediterranean, blockaded the Bosporus and carried out attacks on the Venetian quarter in Constantinople and the Venetian ports on Crete. The economy of Venice was crippled so it had to retaliate, and in 1294, it sent ships out.

Marco Polo, after his return to Venice, led one of Venice's galleys, but in 1298 he was captured and sent to prison in Genoa. He was released the following year after the war ended tentatively with Genoa considered victorious. While in prison, he met Rustichello of Pisa, a writer of romances and the two of them wrote the story we now know as 'The Travels of Marco Polo,' much of which Rustichello considered to be gibberish. The original copy did not survive but the thirst for knowledge about the East meant that lots of copies were made by lots of people and some of them edited Marco Polo's words quite a bit; especially Catholic priests who did not appreciate what Polo had to say about sexual habits or the level of development the "idolaters" of the East had reached.

Marco Polo died in 1324, aged 70. In 1300, a year after he was released from the prison in Genoa, he married Donata Badoer, a noble woman of some wealth and stature and subsequently fathered three daughters (recent discoveries make the claim he had another daughter before he married Donata and went to prison but Marco Polo certainly made no mention of this). I cannot say whether he died a happy man; given his life achievements and loving family I certainly would have. Yet, he did not gain the recognition he was due. His life's story, synthesized in the writings of Rustichello, was not recognized by the majority of his compatriots. They did not believe what he had to say about the Far East. They mockingly called him Il Millione because what he had described in that book told tales of unimaginable grandeur and they figured it was the product of his imagination; the only true millions they surmised were the million lies he had told. What made the case of the non-believers stronger was the fact that he did describe places we know he'd never been to: Japan, Russia's extreme north, the islands of Zanzibar and Madagascar, and the kingdoms of Abyssinia and Aden and in all of these he did describe things he had heard of (that later proved to be true) but were nevertheless hard to believe. We now know most things he wrote about were factual and ironically the parts that his compatriots believed (e.g. for Prester John and the existence of unicorns and griffins) were not. Marco knew what he saw and did not fold before the masses who mocked him. And on his death bed he stated that he'd actually not shared everything for he had seen things that were even more unbelievable.

*"I did not tell half of what I saw, for I knew I would not be believed!"*

**Marco Polo**
*1324*

# THE AFTERMATH

In 1324, when Marco Polo passed away, the Mongol Empire was clearly no longer the menacing force it once was. It had completely splintered into four different parts and each had its separate set of problems. Kublai Khan was followed by a string of khans all of whom mostly did not make it to their 35th birthdays due to assassinations or alcohol induced deaths (starting with his grandson Temur Oljeitu). Kublai's policies of helping the people through bad seasons with crops, animals and tax exemptions were not abandoned but the 1300s began with the Little Ice Age. It brought massive disruption in agriculture and then famines across Eurasia with unexpected frosts, droughts, locusts and typhoons destroying crops everywhere. This along with unsuccessful attempts at invasion of Japan and rampant corruption in Khanbaliq emptied the Mongol treasury within a decade of Kublai's death. Economic calamity, debased currency and succession chaos ensued until in 1333 Toghon Temur inherited the Mongol throne for three decades; but then he became the last ruler of the Yuan dynasty in Beijing. His reign continued amidst floods, droughts, famines and internal strife; the Chinese and Mongols grew alienated with the Chinese prohibited from studying Mongol language and from taking high administrative posts; taxes were raised; citizens were prohibited from owning horses and arms; and the court grew paranoid often reacting with violence to rumors about impending unrest. Ultimately they did not succeed and by the 1350s China was in open rebellion known as the Red Turban movement; it eventually brought the downfall of the Yuan dynasty and Mongol rule, and replaced it with the Ming dynasty and Chinese rule.

The Golden Horde's story proved more stable if far less glamorous. Stability in the steppes was ensured by dividing the peoples into separate uluses of 1,000 people (with farm animals) subjected to the Mongol elite (descendants of the Khan or generals). This prevented anyone local from amassing an army that could challenge the central authority at Sarai; it also settled the nomadic tribes, and diminished banditry that threatened trade flows. Political stability and favorable climate conditions changed the landscape from tough horse-riding tribes, constantly migrating for pastures and constantly warring amongst themselves, to agrarian small settlements that produced a variety of crops and animals (notably excellent horses). Between overland trade revenues and exports of agricultural products (and slaves), the Golden Horde met the 14th century in good shape. Unfortunately, the same weather changes that ravaged the Yuan dynasty brought endless droughts, and so precipitation in the steppes quickly deteriorated. The process sped up after 1320 when vast tracts of land began to gradually turn from poor pastures to outright deserts. Destitute people looked for shelter in cities, which quickly became overcrowded and under-supplied. Then came the Black Plague. And more strife.

The Golden Horde descended into decades of chaos after 1360, when the last princes of the line of Batu killed each other and the throne went up for grabs. Taking advantage of this chaos, the Grand Duchy of Lithuania took over the western reaches of the empire, seizing the Horde's more productive and rich lands in modern-day Belarus and Ukraine. Then the Rus principalities began asserting themselves in the north by first stopping to pay tribute and then facing off or even fighting emissaries. To the east, a newly born Timurid Empire was also encroaching on the Horde's lands and so the next four decades were marked by constant skirmishes with changing success with Lithuania, the Timurids and the Rus principalities (notably Moscow). Eventually the Golden Horde began breaking into its constituent parts predominantly due to poor leadership after 1419[34]. Rival leaders established their own khanates in Central Asia, western Siberia, around the Caspian Sea and in Crimea. Still, it took nearly a century for the vast land empire to completely disintegrate[35]; and then another one for Moscow (that emerged as the dominant Rus principality) to fill in the void that was left (with the 1582 conquest of Siberia).

---

[34] Two khans in those four decades, Tokthamysh and Edigu, were considered to be the leaders who prevented the empire from falling apart even earlier; both Khans were aided to power by Timur, the founder of the Timurid Empire.

[35] Disintegration began almost immediately after Edigu's death in 1419, but there was still a Golden Horde Khanate (subsequently called Great Horde), and its last ruler perished in 1502. A modern view among historians is that the Crimean Khanate (an Ottoman vassal), which lasted well into the 18th century, can be considered the Horde's successor state. I find this to be a technicality. The Golden Horde was done with.

The Ilkhanate saw several decades of relative stability but by 1336 it had succumbed to internal strife and civil war. Conversion to Islam, abandonment of Mongol traditions, and failure to produce a clear succession line (according to some due to inbreeding and excessive alcoholism) alienated the Ilkhan court from the powerful Mongol generals. This resulted in the eventual breakup of the Ilkhanate into separate fiefdoms, led by different warlords; the onset of the Black Death no doubt helped with that too. The official Ilkhanate court in Tabriz carried on until 1353 but it lacked real power. In the Chagatai Khanate, the early decades of the 1300's were marred in quick successions of short-lived khans, and serious tensions between the nomads who lived by the old ways to the east, and the Muslim converts who occupied the rich markets in Transoxiana in the west. The rift was so strong that by the late 1340s, the Chagatai Khanate split in two and while the eastern part (known as Moghulistan) eventually also converted to Islam, it remained split into minor khanates and mostly nomadic.

In Transoxiana meanwhile, a ruler known in the English-speaking world as Timur or Tamerlane who was not of Genghis Khan's bloodline (and perhaps not even a Mongol), rose to power and formed the Timurid Empire. He proved to be a great military leader who never suffered defeat and really deserves a separate book as his conquests set the stage for what became known as the Islamic gunpowder empires (Ottoman, Safavid and Mughal). Although it is said that Timur dreamt of reviving the Mongol Empire, he was not very interested in the poor eastern lands that split off the Chagatai Khanate (and whence the Mongols came originally). Instead, after making Samarkand his capital and consolidating his power over Transoxiana (including by marrying a Genghis line princess), he went after the rich but troubled lands of the former Ilkhanate in Persia. It took him around fifteen years to take all the remnant fiefdoms of the Ilkhanate, one by one, excluding the Turkic beyliks that had formed in Anatolia. And in those 15 years, he also campaigned against the Golden Horde (whose new ruler Tokthamysh, whom he'd helped impose, turned against him), and Moghulistan (who had the indecency to ally with Tokhtamysh); he won both campaigns but wittingly did not pursue occupation of the vast expanses of the Russian or Mongolian steppes[36]. He went to northern India instead, known at the time as the Delhi Sultanate: it was close to Timur's seat of power in Transoxiana, it was split and caught in a decade-long succession turmoil, and it was also considered the richest empire on the planet. He sacked and destroyed Delhi but again did not occupy as he strategically saw a more dangerous rival rising in western Anatolia: the Ottomans.

One of the prevalent historic narratives is that the Ottomans were refugees of the Turkic Kayi tribe, from the lands of modern-day Turkmenistan. They came in droves to Anatolia in the early decades of the 13th century while fleeing the Mongol invasions of Genghis Khan. Many of them became ghazi warriors (plundering non-Muslims) in the employ of the Sultanate of Rum (which was the remnants of the Seljuk Empire, surviving in the central and eastern Anatolian hills). It so happened that for their military services, the Kayi were allowed to settle near the recently formed Nicaean Kingdom in northwestern Anatolia, where they became a constant nuisance for the Christian Nicaeans. The Kayi were

---

[36] In truth, Tokthamysh returned with a vengeance later, but was defeated again, and the Golden Horde never really recovered after this.

subjects to the Seljuk Sultanate of Rum but that became part of the Ilkhanate in 1243 as general Baiju annexed it while Batu Khan was subjugating Constantinople on the other side of the Straits. As the Kayi were on the outskirts of the Sultanate of Rum and not much troubled by Baiju's army, refugees including scholars, craftsmen and merchants would flee to their lands (known as Kayi-uc Beylik or the Kayi Principality in Turkic); so they quickly became a vibrant, skilled and moderately wealthy society. After the re-capture of Constantinople by Michael VIII Palaiologos in 1261 and his re-establishment of the Byzantine Empire, former Nicaean territories in northwestern Anatolia were neglected, abandoned and in fact even stripped off their wealth to rebuild Byzantium and to fund wars on the European mainland. Then in the 1280s, after the death of Michael VIII, the Kayi Turks led by Osman I began to slowly encroach on Nicaean lands while the Byzantines left there proved unable (surprise surprise!) to fend them off. When the Ilkhanate weakened towards the end of the 13th century, Turkic beyliks started declaring independence in 1296; the now Ottoman[37] Beylik did it in 1299.

By 1354, when the Ilkhanate ceased to exist officially, the Ottomans held northwestern Anatolia and had secured the entire south coast of the Sea of Marmara, plus Gallipoli on the other side of the Dardanelles. This meant all of Constantinople's trade was at their mercy (though it is not clear if they extracted any concessions out of this at the time). By 1398 when Timur raided Delhi, the Ottoman Empire, which started as a small principality in the northwest corner of Anatolia, had secured most of the

---

[37] The word Ottoman is a mispronunciation of Osman's name, which sounds like Uthman in Arabian. Ottoman Turks means Osman's Turks.

Anatolian and Balkan peninsulas, defeated a crusading attempt to rescue Bulgaria and completely surrounded Constantinople. And those Turkic beyliks in eastern Anatolia that Timur missed in the Ilkhanate a few decades beforehand came united under Ottoman rule. This coincided with a time of regency (and, yes, strife) in the Mamluk empire, which in Timur's eyes was the only other significant force left in the region. So Timur went back, routed the Ottomans at Sivas in eastern Anatolia and took over Mamluk Syria, while at it. It was in fact, his campaign that broke up a 1399 siege the Ottomans had laid on Constantinople. After Syria Timur continued his anti-Ottoman campaign until he captured and killed their sultan Bayezid I at the Battle of Ankara in 1402; he then sacked the rest of Anatolia all the way to Bursa near the Sea of Marmara and Smyrna (now Izmir) on the Aegean coast. Although Timur chose to withdraw from Anatolia (and died in 1405), this nearly ended the House of Osman as it plunged the Ottomans into a civil war of succession that lasted for over a decade; it also delayed their capture of Constantinople by about 50 years.

Constantinople nevertheless fell to the Ottomans in 1453 and what used to be the major overland trade route into Europe was cut off. The Genoese in Crimea lost everything. All the goods coming in from Asia now had to use the alternative supply routes through the Levantine coast or the Red Sea; these were all in Mamluk hands and under a Venetian monopoly. Volumes dwindled and prices rose big time. Spices like pepper, ginger, cinnamon, nutmeg, cloves, cassia, mace and others all used to be more expensive than gold before the fall of Constantinople but now became unaffordable. Same went for all other Asian goods like silk, tea, porcelain, dies, cotton, sugar, etc. Europe was facing a severe economic crisis, but by this time Portugal, unwilling to put up with the monopolies of Venice and Genoa, had begun exploration for alternative spice routes through the Atlantic. With deep water navigation in its nascent stage, the Portuguese spent over half a century trying to round Africa, fighting circular currents (gyres) not yet well understood. At about the time they finally made it, the Spaniards, backed by Genoese capital, stumbled upon the Americas (though they were quite unhappy with them initially).

The Silk Road gradually became irrelevant as deep water mobility outstripped overland mobility by far. When it comes to trade and the movement of bulk cargo, it is much cheaper and more efficient to move it from the other side of the world by a large sea faring vessel than by a caravan of mules or camels. But the trick wasn't only to learn how to navigate; you also needed to secure the sea lanes. That necessity gave rise to Europe's sea empires who came to dominate the world (in relatively short order) as they commanded sea commerce with their naval superiority and amassed immense wealth. Both the Portuguese and Spanish empires were eventually overcome by countries with superior technology, demography, leadership and geopolitical positions: first the Dutch and later the British and French empires who vied for influence over Europe all the way until things came to a head in the 20th century.

# ... It Truly Rhymes Mr. Twain!

Nowadays, the lands that used to be ruled by the Yuan dynasty are dominated by China and ruled by Beijing. And ruled they are by such grass level control through modern technologies that George Orwell would have watched in dismay. The court in Khanbaliq (called presently Beijing) does not require its subjects to write their names and count-of-stock they have on the front door. The new Great Khan's court knows everything about you better than some members of your household. With modern sensors, big data and AI, his court will soon know if you have diarrhea before you begin to first (nervously) look for a toilet; and it will surely know if you decide that you look good in a red turban. The Zhōng Guó Gòng Chǎn Dǎng[38] dynasty, or the Dang dynasty for short, has now ruled unperturbed for three quarters of a century; it was in the habit of changing khans every five or ten years but the one that was elected during their 18th kurultai in 2012 is so great that in 2022 the realm finally returned to normality and he got the right to rule for life. A big chunk of the Mongol lands, the Tarim basin, Tibet and Manchuria all fall under direct Beijing rule today; and there is heavy influence over the northern parts of the Goryeon Peninsula, some of the less developed peoples of Indochina (notably Myanmar) and Pakistan (carved off Chagatai and Indian lands). The dynasty trades and invests heavily across the world and the economy is great again.

---

[38] This should mean "the Communist Party of China", with "dang" meaning party.

The lands of the Golden Horde were gradually subdued and united again by a new horde from Moscow – European in looks but Mongol in mentality (though less tolerant of foreign culture and religion). Unlike the Golden Horde, they overtook and to this day control the winter lands north and east all the way to the seashores. Like Kublai Khan, Peter of the Romanov dynasty (at the Horde's throne for three centuries), built his great new capital from scratch, but named it after himself. His dynasty tried to emulate the Europeans, since they became masters of the sea and of the world's trade and riches, but that didn't quite work; no matter who ruled the Horde's lands, it was and still is at odds with Europe most of the time. In the 19th century they overpowered and subjugated the better parts of the Chagatai Khanate, including Transoxiana; they snatched the Caucasus kingdoms of Azerbaijan, Georgia and Armenia from the Ilkhanate; and they even extended their territory into Europe's Poland. The Europeans, though more advanced at every level, were scared because they could not subdue the Horde's lands; those lands were vast and the seat of power always endured. That gave Moscow strength and strategic depth that the Europeans lacked. In the 1940s they ventured deeper into Europe like Batu did in the 1240s and with similar results: they ravaged the lands and the peoples who lived in them and then left (though it took them longer than it took Batu Khan to realize they didn't belong there). Still, they retreated east of the Carpathians and continued to be a threat.

Economically however, things were never good. They did not have the sea access the Europeans enjoyed and remained economically, scientifically and technologically backward.

Across the Horde's land, the Romanovs did not have their uluses as equally divided as in the Golden Horde days and at one point the people from the uluses rose up against their masters and tried to re-divide the land's riches more equally. That didn't quite work either, though it took them the good part of a century to realize it. Now, like in the 13th century, their economy is nothing like the Yuan dynasty's especially when the latter was open to trade; so, like in the 13th century, they live off the riches of the lands they control, though modern economies require more than cattle and wheat so they also mine the resources they have below the ground. And like the Horde, in times of economic duress, they have a tendency to break into different khanates. It actually happened again three decades ago with the Chagataids, the Caucasians, the Crimean Khanate, and the Baltic principalities splitting off.

The Ilkhanate's subjects remained deeply religious and into Islam though they adopted a different brand after the fall of the Timurid empire. They lost the western lowlands of Mesopotamia to the Ottoman Turks and remained secluded in the eastern highlands but always had a keen eye on returning to greatness by subjugating the lowlands to their west. On occasion they had some success and did expand west and also east into Afghanistan as well as north into the Caucasus and Transoxiana; but their expansions were quickly rolled back by foreign powers. After the Ottoman Empire crumbled, Mesopotamia and Syria fell into the hands of the Europeans, then succumbed to dictatorships that were sponsored by the Moscow Horde and eventually (after an ill-advised American intervention 20 years ago) succumbed to chaos. This gave the Ilkhanate nowadays an

174

opportunity it had not had in centuries and it took it (though strictly speaking modern empires rely on influence rather than outright subjugation, which makes their outlines on a map somewhat harder). The Ilkhanate has for the last (almost) half a century evolved into a form of a caliphate dictatorship, hostile to the Western powers and particularly to America, so it is excluded from their trading networks; it nevertheless grew into a very influential regional force into Mesopotamia and the Levant.

After the Silk Road was made redundant by the European ships, the Chagatai Khanate remained isolated and economically backward because goods no longer traded through it. Parts of it remained independent for a while but eventually were snatched by either of the three other khanates. The eastern part as mentioned became a part of the Dang dynasty and still is; others were first part of the Ilkhanate, then the Moscow Horde and then they broke off, split into five different khanates nowadays. Only one khan was great enough to have a gilded statue raised while he was still living and in power: the khan of Turkmenistan, who was not really the nation's khan but the nation's father[39]. And this is the only khanate that remained loyal to the old ways of having the throne passed as an heirloom (so no kurultai there). There are some arguments within far corners of this khanate as to whether this great khan deserved the honor of having a (gilded!) statue erected for him while still alive; outside the khanate there is no disagreement that he didn't! The five khanates are weak and divided and they are different from each other: some small, some large, some rich, some poor, some more

---

[39] He did name himself Turkmenbashi, which means Father of the Turkmen.

independent-minded, some subservient, some participating in regional alliances, some not; but all are heavily autocratic, mind-bogglingly corrupt and mostly living off their lands' riches. They were left off the global trading system for being landlocked but would like to see the glorious days of the Silk Road return.

And so would the Great Khan of the Dang dynasty.

In the 19th century, those pesky Europeans and their American offshoots (let's call them all Westerners) used their naval supremacy to encroach on the Chinese coast. The then ruling Qing dynasty was weakened, following decades of famines, rebellions and wars (not exactly like the 1300s but rhyming). The Westerners wreaked havoc, imposed their rules, reaped economic benefits, controlled seaports and had spheres of influence, sometimes threatening the Emperor himself; it was a century of humiliation. The situation in the Ilkhanate was similar as they practically controlled the ruling court there. They also tried to subdue the Horde several times but as it turned out, its lands were naturally secluded from the sea and it was too big for them to succeed on land[40]. Eventually those sea powers began fighting amongst themselves because they were divided in their land bases in Europe. So fiercely they fought that they ended up destroying their powerful empires to a point where the Horde (which already included the Chagataids) could attack them back and attempt to subdue them. It would have succeeded too if it was not for the Americans who were strong and secure in their land base. They managed to salvage most European maritime states plus a few

---

[40] It did, in fact, take lands from both the Qing dynasty and the Ilkhanate in this century, and had its own spheres of influence.

others but all Europeans had now become too weak to sustain their powerful navies and compete in the seas; thus only the Americans remained supreme rulers and protectors of the sea trade and the maritime states.

They contained the Horde in its landlocked domain and excluded it from their trading system. At the same time the Dang dynasty rose to power and expelled all sea powers from its land; consequently, it was also excluded from their trading system. A few decades later the Ilkhanate also expelled the Westerners and was also excluded from their trading system. Around that time however, the Dang dynasty had a new khan who decided he could use this trading system to enrich the dynasty and make it great. The Westerners on the other hand needed him to side with them against the powerful menacing Horde (which had acquired some European vassal states and had strong influence in others not only in Europe but around the world as well). So the Westerners let the Dangs in and the economy boomed, putting the dynasty squarely on a path to greatness.

Economic exclusion eventually brought the Horde down. And it began to break up. To the dismay of the court in Moscow, not only its vassal states but many of its very own subjects (particularly the khanates in its western reaches), preferred to have property rights, rule of law, freedom of speech, a say in who should govern them, and a higher standard of living: all of them were thus lured by the sea powers who could offer these luxuries. Imagine the nerve ... outrageous!!! It turned out most of them did not care to have the honor of being a proud property of the khan, bravely facing the enemy! They did not care to strive to get into the uniformed or security castes (and live like lesser men if deemed unfit)! They did not appreciate the convenience of having the state choose what you need, take decisions for you and bear the burden of property. They even sacrificed traditional values like racism, chauvinism or the right to beat the crap out of your wife! These people did not understand that a natural born leader would know better than them and would without a doubt take good care of them! They preferred instead some mumbo-jumbo western propaganda called "democracy"!!! And started breaking away from the Horde and worse: joining forces with the Westerners.

Thankfully, a new strong khan rose to power in Moscow and started to roll things back. He consolidated power in the steppes, in Siberia and in the Volga basin. He managed to bring back the Chagataids who were too far away and landlocked for the Westerners to influence anyway. And he enforced some success in the Caucasus. But despite his attempts, the Crimean Khanate proved a tough nut to crack: it was fooled into democracy too! The Westerners are now helping it to break away for good and have again excluded the Horde from the trading system.

But now, the Westerners began worrying about the Dang's economic success and growing power as well. Some even accused it of having imperial expansion designs and began turning hostile. A peculiar situation emerged: animosity with the Westerners put together three autocratic powers – the Dang dynasty, the (weakened) Moscow Horde, and the Ilkhanate – along with the Chagataids trapped in between them. Should they form a Beijing-lead strategic alliance (not an empire, please!), it also seems reasonable to imagine that the northern part of Goryeo, the Pagan Kingdom in Myanmar, Pakistan, Mesopotamia, and Syria will all join them; India is too large and too anti-China to be considered. It is such a strange coincidence that if you were to paint it with the same color on a map, such an alliance would look a lot like the the Mongol Empire of old. And it already has the perfect physical axis to rotate around (sorry, not axis!!!): the new Silk Road, now called the Belt and Road Initiative (BRI).

That initiative is obviously a purely economical project and nothing to do with empire building, as the Great Khan has underlined hundreds of times. It is simply meant as an alternative means to supply critical resources needed for the economy (not like rounding the Cape of Good Hope!!); it will have the added benefit of bringing Chinese capital, higher technology, premium products, and superior management practices to the source countries (not like the British or Dutch East India Companies!!); it will develop critical overland routes, which will be an expensive but fruitful undertaking (not like the Berlin-Baghdad railway the Germans wanted to build before World War 1!!); it will spread the ideology of socialism with Chinese characteristics, which basically means business and state working together for the greater good (No! Not like fascism!! The definition of fascism is "a governmental system led by a dictator having complete power, forcibly suppressing opposition and criticism, regimenting all industry, commerce, etc., and emphasizing an aggressive nationalism and often racism"). Now, why would you think that what was once made in Europe, could later be made in China?

Rhymes? Here's another one from Mark Twain: he said he went bankrupt at first slowly, and then all at once. Just please don't think of the dollar, which is the only thing underwriting the US military, which in turn is the only thing standing in the way of a potentially devastating steamroller a few decades from now … think of the British pound or the Dutch gulden[41]. I bet this time is different … just not sure if it will rhyme?

To be continued…

---

[41] Ray Dalio has a lot to say in that regard. His book "Principles for Dealing with the Changing World Order", published in 2021, is an amazing, though quite a chilling read!

# IN THE WORKS

## The Age of Discovery Series

This book is intended to be the first volume in a series centred on the Age of Discovery that would span almost the entire modern world history from the 13th to the 20th century. The modern world that we find ourselves living in has been shaped in large part by the exploits of travelers who ventured out into the unknown and overcame dangers and hardship beyond anything we can encounter in our day and age. The significance of their achievements is often underestimated, since it is in the human nature to see events from a modern-world point of view and to take things like contemporary levels of education, means of communication, or available medicines for granted. But I find that readers who have a keen interest in history also possess an extraordinary level of intelligence and imagination, which helps them to appreciate the truly fascinating stories behind their adventures and the historic events that shaped their lives.

Future books are set to cover the lives and exploits of Columbus, Magellan, da Gama, Cortes, Jan Huygen, Tasman, Drake, Bering, Livingston, James Cook, Amundsen, and many more. They will cover the rise and fall of European and Asian empires, the wars of independence in the Americas, the slave trade and the advents of capitalism and the Industrial Revolution. I also plan a prequel depicting the history of the Vikings and a subset on the Golden Age of Piracy in the Caribbean. I have already begun work on Volume II, which narrates the life story of a man who is often neglected as a second to Marco Polo but whose life was spent on the road, travelling far and wide across Eurasia and Africa. And he did it just for the sake of traveling.

## Vol II: Ibn Battuta

So, if Marco Polo was one of the world's greatest travelers, then surely Ibn Battuta (or Abu Abdullah Muhammad Ibn Battuta to give him his full name) was THE greatest traveler in pre-modern times. Whereas Polo traveled 15,000 miles, Battuta managed an extraordinary 73,000 miles – or 117,000 kilometers – over a thirty-year period, extensively in Eurasia and Africa. As Marco Polo produced manuscripts of his travels, so Battuta did the same, dictating his memories for a book that is now known in modern terms as The Rihla. Despite his life, it is with surprise and sadness that his name is barely known in the modern world, yet his achievements were beyond anything that can be understood today. If he is ever referred to now, it is normally in a patronizing 'Islamic Marco Polo' reference, which doesn't do him justice at all.

Marco Polo was, without a doubt, a great traveler and explorer who brought back to Europe an invaluable account of the Mongol Empire and the Far East in general. But we should not forget that he set out on a journey his father and uncle had already made (they had to take a different course due to an unexpected war); and there was a particular purpose to it: trade. He spent 17 years in the employ of Kublai, so if we are to describe Polo by today's standards, we would think of him as an émigré who works on the other side of the world.

Battuta traveled for the sake of traveling. He set out for pilgrimage but kept on going. He traveled across Eurasia and only returned to his hometown after 24 years and after he had visited Mecca four times (so not one but four pilgrimages). And then he left again. He did not trade and did not seek wealth but was instead sponsored by people he met along the road like local rulers and various wealthy individuals. And unlike Marco Polo who seemingly wrote the book with the help of Rustichello without prior intent to do so, Battuta explicitly chronicled his journey from the start. So if we are to describe him by today's standards, we would think of him as a travel blogger who seeks sponsorship to fund his travels.

He was born in 1304 in Tangier, so five years after Marco Polo was released from his Genoan prison and set out on a pilgrimage in 1325 when he was 21. He traveled through the Maghreb, Egypt, the Nile, the Arabian Peninsula, Persia, Anatolia, Central Asia, India, Southeast Asia, China, Spain and Mali. His itinerary is outstanding and he lived to tell his story. He traveled through the Ilkhanate in tumultuous times, which eventually led to its disintegration and just like Marco Polo, was affected by historic and geopolitical events that brought about epochal changes and deserve to be explored in depth. Just like one cannot understand the story of Marco Polo (and family) without understanding the story of the Silk Road and the Mongol Empire, so too one cannot understand the story of Ibn Battuta without understanding the story behind the Islamic Caliphate and the forces that converged to bring about its prolonged decline: Seljuks, Mamluks, Crusaders, Mongols and Reconquista.

He was of Berber descent, meaning he was part of an ethnic group indigenous to Barbary or the west part of the North African coast. His childhood was seemingly spent studying Islam as part of the Maliki jurisprudence school, a strict understanding of the faith. It wasn't until he was 21, in June 1325, that he made his pilgrimage to Mecca. This was a journey that ordinarily would take around sixteen months, but he made it his plan to travel as far as possible and experience lands that were far away. He wouldn't return to Morocco for twenty-four years.

Chronicling his journeys would take a whole book in itself, and it reads like the most expensive itinerary ever, but the list seems almost endless. For a quick and brief look, these are the places he visited, stayed in, worked in, revisited, fell in love, fell out of love and referred to in his book. Extensive travels in North Africa, Iraq and Iran, Arabia and Somalia, Swahili, Anatolia, Central Asia and the Indian subcontinent, Southeast Asia and China, Spain and Mali and Timbuktu. These are just a handful of destinations that had their own adventures individually.

He visited Mecca three times, and even after his return to Tangier, where he heard that his father had died fifteen years previously, and his mother more recently, he went traveling for another five years. When he was at the early stage of his journeys, after a mere 2,200 miles, he met two very pious men who both predicted his future. Sheikh Burhanuddin, who prophesied he would travel to India, Sind and China, where he would meet three of his brothers. The second, Sheikh Mursidi interpreted a dream about Battuta, where it was said he would become the world's greatest traveler. Maybe the story has been lost in translation down the centuries, but these types of prophecies were taken extremely seriously at that time. A personal map of the future was being prepared for him.

The danger of traveling alone was clear, so he regularly would join caravans of pilgrimages, until he decided that he would take his own path. Long and lonely days followed, but there is no evidence to suggest that he was at the behest of any particular danger. It was an extraordinary decision though, to abandon a type of safety for the freedom of unplanned travel.

He also married numerous times, in the habit of taking a wife when he arrived at a new destination, and then divorcing her when he left. It seems a little harsh in our modern-day thinking, and at one stage he had four wives, but this was something that was normally accepted. He also fathered many children.

It has been suggested that he made no notes on his travels, so the book that is attributed to him – its full title being 'A Masterpiece To Those Who Contemplate The Wonders Of Cities And The Marvels Of Travelling' which is far more manageable as The Travels or The Rihla - has its critics. Some scholars have accused him of plagiarism and suggested that he didn't actually travel to all of the places listed, especially China as timeline chronology is at odds with history. Whatever, his traveling is legendary, and maybe the controversy over his publication is a reason for him being virtually forgotten now, compared to Marco Polo especially. He died in 1369 and left behind a huge legacy. Even if the book isn't as accurate as hoped for, he has given historians a unique look into 14th century Islam and the countries he visited.

Few know of him today, but a shopping mall in Dubai plays host to his name and a large tableau of his life and travels is prominent, and of course the Tangier Ibn Battuta airport is named after him. It seems like a small reward for a life lived beyond the norm.

# FROM THE AUTHOR

Dear Reader,

Thank you very much for acquiring and reading my book! I hope you have enjoyed it!

I have always been passionate about history and travel, so I greatly enjoyed writing this manuscript, although I was surprised by the effort and time it took, particularly around publishing and marketing. As an independent publisher, I have to be more involved in this process and accordingly shift my focus from research and writing to publishing and promotion. Putting it all together was hard work but in the end, the joy of my readers' appreciation makes it more than worthwhile!

Reader reviews are the single most important element that helps build an author and provides invaluable feedback and connection to their readers. They also provide other readers with similar interests and passions with an insight, they otherwise cannot have.

I would therefore be very grateful if you could spare a minute or so of your time to share your honest feedback by using the hyperlinks or QR codes below. This will be of great value to me and I will wholly appreciate it, read it, and contemplate it!

If you would like to leave a review
please visit my BOOK REVIEW PAGE

Amazon.com review page -- USA
Amazon..co.uk review page -- UK
Amazon.au review page -- AUSTRALIA
Amazon.ca review page -- CANADA
Amazon.jp review page -- JAPAN
Amazon.in review page -- INDIA
Amazon.de review page -- GERMANY
Amazon.nl review page -- NETHERLANDS
Amazon.fr review page -- FRANCE
Amazon.it review page -- ITALY
Amazon.es review page -- SPAIN
Amazon.mx review page -- MEXICO
Amazon.br review page -- BRAZIL

Or scan this QR code if you have a paperback copy

Many thanks and best regards,

J.L. Roger